CUPIDS ENCHANTMENT

NAUGHTY CUPID SERIES ANNIVERSARY EDITION

MICHELLE M PILLOW

MICHELLEPILLOW.COM

Cupid's Enchantment
Paranormal Fantasy Romance
Naughty Cupid Book One

Contrary to popular belief, Cupid is not a cute little cherub. And he'll take revenge on any who say differently. Just ask Ilar, Commander of the Lycaon guard...

Lady Rhiannon's beauty is distracting suitors from her older sister and ruining her chances at marriage, so her father has her locked her away in a tower. Believing she is going crazy from the isolation, Rhiannon hears a frightful voice. The next thing she knows, she wakes up in a strange forest pursued by mythical wolf men. And, worst of all, their leader is taking her home with him.

Ilar is irritated to discover an enchanted female—a

human, their ancient hunters—disrupting his Lycan Guards. One sniff of this mortal's enchantment and the men go insane, trying to kill each other for her hand. Ilar has no choice but to break the spell by claiming the female as his own. But who knows what will happen when Cupid's Enchantment is broken?

Author recommends reading books in order of release. For details please visit www.michellepillow.com

To those who don't like Valentine's Day—a Cupid even you can love.

Cupid's Enchantment
Cupid's Revenge
Cupid's Favor

The Playful Prince
The Bound Prince
The Rogue Prince
The Pirate Prince

Qurilixen Lords
Dragon Prince
More Coming Soon!

Captured by a Dragon-Shifter Series
Determined Prince
Rebellious Prince
Stranded with the Cajun
Hunted by the Dragon
Mischievous Prince
Headstrong Prince

Space Lords Series
His Frost Maiden
His Fire Maiden

His Metal Maiden

His Earth Maiden

His Woodland Maiden

Dynasty Lords Series

Seduction of the Phoenix

Temptation of the Butterfly

Having trouble finding the books?

Updated Buy Links Here

To learn more about the Qurilixen World series of books
and to stay up to date on the latest book list visit
www.MichellePillow.com

CUPID WAS LIVID. NO, HE WAS OUTRAGED. HE WAS beyond furious.

Make fun of him, would he? Make the whole court at Lycaon think he was a joke—an incompetent clod that couldn't make two pigs fall in love. Call him a fairy, would he? Call him a rosy-faced cherub? He *accidentally* hit a man instead of a goat with a love dart, causing *one* couple to fall in love four hundred years ago, and he got branded a matchmaker for life.

Bah. Ach.

It was time for the jests to end. Cupid would show them what this squat little *cherub* could do. He'd have the last laugh. He'd prove to them that not only could he make the whole Lycaon court fall in love—he'd make them fall in love with the same woman.

Oh, and this was his favorite part. He'd not get just any woman. He'd bring one from the mortal realm—the ugliest woman he could find. See how the wolves liked panting after a human—their ancient hunters, the whole reason the realms of mortal and magic had been separated in the first place.

His short legs pumped along the dusty, abandoned path coming from his cave home. He angrily kicked at little daisies that dared to grow along the side, ruining the look of his taller weeds. He hated flowers. He hated lycans. And he most definitely hated to watch people fall in love.

Cupid paused in his tirade to look at the vial of bright pink philter in his gnarled troll hand. A wide grin spread over his thick, long lips, lifting under his oversized nose. His small, black eyes lit with greedy pleasure. This potion was old magic. No simple blow dart would do this time. Once he doused the mortal woman with this pheromone, he would bring the entire Lycan Guard howling to their knees.

He'd find a woman for them, all right. Then that overbearing Lord Ilar would never doubt his magic again.

LADY RHIANNON OF WEILSHIRE LOOKED OUT OVER the dismal courtyard of her castle home. The narrow slit in the thick wall made it difficult to see, not that she would've been able to see much from the height of the tall tower anyway. It had been raining for what seemed like weeks, never letting up once as the gray skies consumed the day hours with their dark foreboding. The ground had turned into a bottomless pit of sticky black mud, marred by the heavy tracking of horses and carts. It made for a very bleak view.

Rhiannon had been banished, once again, to spend the day away from her father's guests. Pressing her cheek tightly to the slotted opening, she reached her hand through the thick wall to feel the outside of the castle. A sprinkling of freezing water on her fingertips rewarded her efforts, barely.

Her father, Lord Orrell, was a Welsh Earl who hadn't been blessed with sons. Rhiannon was the younger of two daughters. Agrona, the eldest sister, would marry his heir. It was a serious business, Agrona's marriage, and Lord Orrell didn't want the fairer sibling—again—ruining his chance at a proper alliance.

Rhiannon frowned. She'd offer to cut off her own nose if they'd agree to let her come down from the tower. It wasn't her fault that every one of Agrona's suitors turned to her instead. It's not like she encouraged them or wanted them. Unwed noblemen were a rarity at the moment, and Lord Orrell couldn't afford to bind Rhiannon to one without first ensuring Agrona's future. Rhiannon didn't have any desire to marry and was quite comfortable running around her father's keep—when she was allowed to run around.

With a sigh, she brought her hand back inside. Pressing her nose into the crevice, she sniffed. The cold air hit against her face, stinging her cheeks to a sharp red. She knew she shouldn't stay away from the fire too long, lest she caught her death in the wind. But, as an exceptionally strong draft found its way to her, she smiled, and couldn't quite force herself to move away.

Cupid's beady eyes narrowed in black mischief as he crawled his way over the lively main hall floor. Magic kept him partially hidden, but he didn't want to ruffle the tapestries and make his presence known. Damned humans spooked too easily. If it had been any other time, he would have gladly stirred up a mischievous wind just to watch them run away.

Help. Help. The devil approaches anon, he mimicked.

He heard the cackling of his own pleasure in his head as he thought of the mortal cries. He almost chuckled aloud in his good humor. He knew he wasn't supposed to be in the mortal realm, but damned if it wasn't too much fun.

Then, shaking his head, he thought, *Bah. Foolish humans. Anything unexplained is the devil.*

Pressing his long lips together, he searched the hall for the most horrendous of the mortal women. As he eyed the head table, his heart about stopped. A dreamy smile came to the troll's crinkled lips, and he smacked them together.

Now, there's a tasty little treat, he thought, as he stared at the large goddess at the high table. A touch of drool spilled over the side of his mouth, dripping to the floor like thick tree sap.

A torch burned brightly behind the woman's head, making the frizzy strands of her most beautiful hair stick out like a banshee. She was wrapped in yards of clashing yellow silk. Her nose hooked at the end in the most enjoyable way and the giant mole on her chin had a glorious three hairs growing out of it. Three! The luckiest of numbers when it came to hairs and moles.

Cupid sighed dreamily, loving the pull of her one eyebrow dipping over her narrow eyes. Musicians played a lively tune, but Cupid couldn't hear them over the frantic beating of his pea-sized heart. She was perhaps the most enchanting mortal he'd ever seen. Ah, but the fair temptress wouldn't be going with him this night. She was too beautiful, and he was in search of an ugly maiden—the most repugnant female he could find.

"Aye, he keeps 'er locked away in the tower," Cupid

heard a burly man whisper. The troll stopped, changing his route to near a table of knights.

The soldier who spoke tore a chunk of meat off a bone and then threw the scrap over his shoulder. It landed on the floor at Cupid's feet. The little troll licked his lips, took the bone up, and gnawed at it in pleasure. These men might be mortals, but they sure knew how to live right.

Cupid perked his tiny ears as he crept closer to listen, the bone hanging halfway out of his lips. He sat beneath the large soldier's bench seat, surrounded by the satisfying perfume of sweaty feet. He continued to gnaw. The mortal court was much better than Lycaon's cleanly ways. Whoever heard of a law stating you must come to the table clean?

Bah. Cupid thought with a repulsed shiver. He'd been kicked out of Lycaon more than once for not bathing.

"Lord Orrell is afraid she'll turn away Lady Agrona's suitors," the knight continued. The men all looked at the high table where Cupid's temptress sat. Her thick lips chewed greedily on a hunk of meat. When she pulled the bite away, the lower half of her face was covered in grease. The men grimaced as they watched the lady.

Cupid sighed. It must be a terrible woman locked in the tower indeed to frighten a suitor away from such a lovely vision of womanly perfection at the high table. And to make grown soldiers shiver at the very thought of her.

Slowly, a smile formed on his wrinkled face. A woman so hideous that she had to be locked away in a tower? A maiden like that was precisely what Cupid needed to avenge himself against Lord Ilar, Commander of the Lycans. Let his whole wolfen army go mad with lust for an unsightly woman. Let Ilar himself fall so madly in love that he would blindly mate with her.

Aye, Cupid mused with enthusiasm. *Let him degrade himself by choosing an ugly mortal for a lifemate. That will teach him the dangers of teasing a troll.*

"ACH. SHE'S UNBEARABLE. TOO SKINNY," CAME A muttering voice.

Rhiannon gasped, pulling her face away from the window. Her heart sped slightly, as she paused to listen. Her nose was frozen red and her eyes watered from the nip of the cold wind. She blinked to clear her vision and looked around the tower bedroom. When all was silent, she let loose her captured breath and laughed at her nervousness. She'd definitely been held captive too long. She was starting to hear voices.

Rhiannon stepped toward the fire to warm her chilled face. She curled her bare feet into the soft fur rug. The thick pelt was already warmed by the fire and felt wonderful against her toes. Closing her eyes, she let the heat wash over her.

"Ach. And she smells so clean."

Rhiannon nearly screamed. She spun on her heels to glance around the chamber. Her bed was empty, completely smoothed. Her trunk was untouched. Other than the chair by the window, there was nothing else.

"What sorcery is this? Who's there?" she asked, her voice shaky. She wound her hand into the blue skirt of her long tunic dress, twisting it up in her floor-length sleeves. Suddenly, her bodice felt a little too tight. She inhaled deeply in an effort to control her breathing and slow her racing heart. She pressed her lips to stop their trembling. "Show yourself to me at once."

Rhiannon bent over to peek beneath the bed. Nothing.

"Oh. The grating voice."

She shot back up.

"Who are you?" she demanded. She worked her hands frantically, nearly ripping the material of her gown. She couldn't tell where the voice originated. It sounded hollow as if coming from all directions of the circular tower. She glanced around for a weapon. There was nothing. "What do you want from me?"

She backed up until the heat of the fire tingled so badly she thought her hair might catch fire. The voice didn't sound like a man, but a rasping monster. For a long moment there was silence, marred only by the raggedness of her breath as she forced air into her constricted lungs.

"Oh," she whimpered softly to herself, hoping to draw some measure of comfort from hearing her own voice. "I think I'm going mad in this seclusion. There's no one here. The chamber is empty. There's no one here…"

"Ah. And she's weak—scared and weak and trembling. Perfect, perfect. The lycans don't like weak." The voice was beside itself in giddy pleasure.

This time Rhiannon did scream as she darted for the door, convinced spirits plagued the castle. The alderman had warned her that unrested souls could walk on such dreary evenings as these. She hadn't believed him at the time.

The door was locked. She wrapped her stiff fingers around the circular handle, pulling viciously at it, shaking her entire body in an attempt to break through the thick oak barrier. It didn't budge, not even to jar with noise. Tears ran down her cheeks, spilling from her frightened eyes. She called for help, pounded hard at the thick wood. There was no answer. She was too far from the hall and her father's men couldn't hear her cries.

Cupid launched a pink vial from behind the ugly woman. She didn't see it as it materialized out of thin air. With a thud it hit her on the back of her skull, breaking into minuscule pieces of glass that disappeared like the last glow of falling ash. The impact of the blow sent her forehead crashing into the door. A soft moan of surprise left her lips as she was instantly knocked unconscious.

Her frail body dropped to the castle floor like a stone, unmoving as she lay distorted at odd angles. The pink potion from the vial spread over her flesh and soaked into her skin, gliding into her mouth, her eyes, her nose. It didn't stop until every last drop vanished as if it had never been there.

Cupid dropped the cloak of magic that hid him from the human world. He ambled forward on his short legs to study his captive, grimacing to see that her skin was soft and rosy and too smooth. He knew her eyes were a disgusting blue beneath her lids and could only be glad that they were closed. Her hair was a curly mass of blonde that reflected the orange of the firelight. If he'd been a younger troll, he might have heaved his supper upon her face.

Too bad, he thought in disgust. *It would be a vast improvement.*

Picking his overlarge nose, he shivered in contemplation. If he was going to have to travel to the realm of the immortals with her as a companion, he needed to do something to hide her hideousness from his view. Hearing the rain, he grinned. Plucking his finger out of his nose, he grabbed the human lady beneath her armpits.

Slowly taking one step back in the tower bedchamber, he dragged her with him. Cupid felt the rain hit upon his hunched shoulders. Another step and he felt the squish of mud beneath his feet. The woman didn't move as he hauled her from the tower bedchamber into the cold storm. With a plop, he dropped her shoulders, and she fell into the muck. The tower bedchamber faded entirely from view.

Cupid looked up at the narrow slit of the tower window high above them and smiled. Ah, he loved magic. There was no need to lug this heavy load down all those stairs. Looking back at the woman, he frowned anew. The sooner he was done with this task the better. Taking revenge had never been so unpleasant a chore.

Rolling the woman over, he covered her motionless body in mud. He slapped it on her face and forced it into her hair, drowning out the disgusting blonde hue. When he'd finished, he smiled. That was much, much better.

4

RHIANNON TOOK A DEEP BREATH, FEELING HER MIND ease from the shadowed darkness of dreams. The images had been more like nightmares. Dark, shapeless figures hunted her. She thought them to be men but for their long beastlike howls. She'd tried to run from them, but they'd been so fast, moving as if they were part of the night itself.

Rhiannon frowned, taking another breath. The air was sweet—too sweet for the tower bedchamber. It smelled like the forest. Her limbs still quivered faintly from the remnant memories of the nightmares. Her mouth was glued shut, her skin tight. Even her eyes didn't want to open from the darkness, no matter how hard she tried to blink.

"Um," she groaned, sitting up. Her closed mouth

muffled the sound. She felt dizzy, as she lifted her fingers to touch her eyes. Dried mud covered her face.

Rhiannon dug and wiped at her eyelids until she managed to free her vision. Looking around, she did her best to ignore the grating of dust in her eyes. She was in a forest, though the trees didn't look like her father's land. They were too tall, too thick at the base, and the bark was too red.

She narrowed her gaze in confusion. Where was she? She couldn't remember a thing. Where was the hunting party? Certainly she had been hunting if she was in the forest. She felt around on the ground. Where was her bow? Was she attacked? Did she lose her seat on her mount and fall? It would explain her dizzy head.

No, she thought with pride. She was much too skilled of a rider for that and, though it ached, her body wasn't terribly bruised.

Hearing water nearby, she struggled to her hands and knees. Disoriented, Rhiannon crawled her way to what blurrily looked like a stream. Kneeling by the shore, she cupped water into her stiff fingers and washed her face, scrubbing hard. The mud was clumped thick and tight. It seemed like an eternity passed before she could get her features clear of it.

Blinking, she looked up at the sky. The purple appeared a little off color for such a beautiful day. Wait.

Hadn't it been raining? That could explain the color. But what of the ground? It was dry, almost cracked where the stream didn't touch it.

Rhiannon felt her stomach churn, growling viciously at her for food. Her throat felt coated in dirt. She leaned back over to cup more water, drinking before continuing to splash her face. She hoped the stream wouldn't have an adverse effect on her stomach. As she rinsed her hands, Rhiannon took a deep breath. She heard another growl and abruptly froze. It wasn't her stomach making the noise.

Her eyes wide, she gradually looked around, careful not to move too quickly. She had no weapon and wouldn't be able to fight off whatever wild beast was nearby. She curled her fingers, retracting them from the chill of the water as they bound into fists.

Behind her the forest was dense—too dense to see through. She noticed the leaves were large and pale. The clear stream cut through the trees, making its own clearing. Along the shores were wide paths. A littering of leaves and twigs covered the dirt floor. Sunlight shone from the break in the trees, glistening like liquid crystals on the top of the glassy water. A log fell over the stream at a shallow point to make a natural bridge between the two shores.

Rhiannon slowly climbed to her feet, sliding on moss

that grew along the water's stony edge. Her feet were bare, and her toes cold and numb. She was stiff and jabs of pain radiated up her legs. The heavy mud on her gown weighed her down as she tried to move. She continued to slip, but she intended on making the bridge and didn't stop to look for better footing.

Whatever growled had been on this side of the stream. She had every intention of getting herself across before it found her. Inching along, she saw a branch and lifted it like a broadsword.

"Rrrrr."

Rhiannon stiffened at the low rumble. Whatever it was came from her left, and it positively wasn't human. She continued to inch as quietly as possible. Angling the branch in the creature's direction, she backed away.

"Rrrrr."

Oh, no. That growl was to the right. She froze, tears of apprehension coming to her scratchy eyes as she awaited another sound.

All of a sudden, a low resonation started around her, coming from the forest like a demonic chorus, rumbling through her body as if the earth shook beneath her feet. Whatever made the noise, the animal wasn't alone. Jerking into action, Rhiannon ran for the bridge. The branch fell from her shaking fingers. To her horror, a large gray wolf jumped out from the trees, blocking her path.

The creature snarled, snapping his sharp teeth to keep her back. The thick fur along its spine stood on end as it postured. Yellow eyes stared at her—dangerous and probing as if it understood more than it should. She thought them too knowledgeable to be the eyes of a wild beast. It was almost as if the wolf calculated her next move.

The first wolf was soon followed by others—all shades of brown and gray. Their bodies were too large to be ordinary wolves or dogs, as they were three times the size of such. They formed a snarling blockade around her, preventing any retreat but to the water. Rhiannon took to the icy stream without a second thought, splashing away from the beast-covered shore, praying the creatures couldn't swim. They inched closer, sniffing at her from the dry land, watching her, wanting her, salivating for her.

Rhiannon cried out in fear. She'd never seen anything like these creatures before. They were terrifying.

Her heart pounded as she hit deeper water. Mud from her dress and hair swirled around her, trailing downstream. The current tried to pull her with it, but she fought it, using every bit of energy she had. Her hair tangled her limbs in a muddy mess and stuck to her face. It was hard going backward, but she didn't dare look away as she paddled her arms and kicked her legs for swifter speed.

The gray wolf crept closer to the shoreline. She could see its nostrils flaring as he touched an oversized paw slowly into the cold water. The others skulked behind him. Rhiannon pumped her limbs faster, whimpering. Her legs intertwined the heavy skirts of the tunic gown. For a moment, she thought she would go under. Her head dipped. The cold stung her limbs, burning her nose.

A dark brown beast lurched forward to jump after her. Rhiannon pumped her limbs faster, fighting to stay up, propelling her body back. A chaos of movement followed the brown wolf's daring. Another, lighter wolf, launched after the bold creature to stop its attack on her. They rolled along the shoreline, snapping and fighting. Soon all the creatures brawled, skirmishing with each other more than looking at her.

As she hit shallow water, Rhiannon braced her feet into the streambed and stood. Turning around, she concentrated on running. Water dripped from her clothes, causing a horrific chill now that the breeze hit upon her wet skin. Her movements were labored from the extra weight of her soaked dress and her dirty hair blocked her vision. She didn't stop to right the locks as she pushed toward the shore.

Rhiannon only made it as far as the edge before she was snatched up by two strong hands on her arms. She yelped in surprise and weakly squirmed against the hold. Her captor shook her until she stilled and then proceeded to haul her forward onto the bank. She was clasped in a vise-like grip, almost bruising in its strength. Her bare feet sank into the muddy shore and her face was inches away from a warm chest.

Slowly, Rhiannon registered that the hands felt human and she was thankful for it. She tried to move her cold body toward the protective warmth. The hands held her away, and she was too frail to resist them. Her head bobbed forward on her neck, her energy almost spent. She gasped for breath, struggling to stay awake.

The man roared like a beast. The sound stirred her from the blackness that crept over her mind. Unexpectedly, the growling stopped, and the forest was again silent.

Rhiannon held very still. The strong hands on her arms gripped her tight, keeping her on her feet. She willed the forest to disappear. This had to be a nightmare. She didn't know where she was. Creatures such as these didn't exist in the real world. If this wasn't a dream, her sanity had snapped. She couldn't be insane. She didn't feel irrational—at least she didn't think she was. Did the crazy know they were insane?

Ugh, this is madness.

Gradually, the silence invaded her, and she calmed. The hands on her arms were stiff, but they didn't threaten or squeeze, merely held. Opening one eye first, she was surprised to see a manly nipple surrounded by tight, bronzed muscle. The other eye soon followed and she couldn't help but stare. Whoever this knight was, he was sturdily built. A strange jolt went through her system upon sensing how close she stood to the stranger.

Lord Ilar, Commander of the Lycan Guard, held the scared female before his naked chest. Seizing her slender arms in his hands, he kept her from running. His eyes blazed with a liquid heat to see the havoc she wrought upon his men. Never had he seen the lycan guards act in such a way, nearly killing each other over a mere female. If she had continued to run, she would only have made matters worse. The lycan enjoyed nothing more than a good chase, and to chase a pleasing, unmated female was the ultimate indulgence.

With a roaring order, he'd told the men to retreat. The woman had jolted at the sound of his harsh voice but he didn't let her go. The lycan guards snarled and snapped at him in protest. But, to Ilar's relief, they obeyed and withdrew into the forest, disappearing into the trees.

Ilar frowned. His men had been ready to fight over this woman and he couldn't imagine what had gotten into them. In all his years as their Commander, he'd never seen them so undisciplined. The guards never battled to such an extent over a female. He'd almost thought it a joke when he heard their anger in his head. The psychic mind link that connected them had risen like never before until Ilar feared his men were under magical assault.

Suddenly, he realized what was happening. A soft scent wafted to him, tempting him with pleasure. He scowled, leaning over to sniff the woman's dirt covered head. Hot desire flooded into his limbs, making his body lurch in instant response. He pulled back, displeased. Something was definitely wrong with her. Maybe it was a magical attack after all.

"Wake up, Rhian, wake up."

Ilar stiffened, hearing the woman's whispered words. Her accent was soft, strange to his ears. She spoke in the old language, one they rarely used but still knew. She closed her eyes tight, at least from what he saw through the veil of her muddied hair. He heard her heart beating in his head, almost deafening in its rapid fear. The sound sparked the hunter in him. He tried to block it out and suppress the impulse.

"Get your lazy arse out of bed, Rhian," she continued in a hushed plea, refusing to move more than a shiver.

Ilar wondered if it was his touch or the cold that made her tremble so. He held her back from his chest when she would naturally lean into him. She was filthy, and he had no desire to soil himself with her.

Her whispering continued, growing frantic, "Begone. Begone."

He wondered if the woman was merely insensible or just crazy. She didn't move, as she stared at his chest. The shivering lessened by small degrees and he hesitated before letting her go. His senses on alert, he kept an eye on her, afraid that she might run.

He couldn't let this woman out of his sight, not with the unnaturally strong pheromones she emitted. She was lucky he'd managed to stop the men from attacking her and each other. He'd seen well their posturing stances. They tried to impress her with their power—not that this woman appeared to understand what they were about.

He wondered if she were an elf. She did have the slight figure of that race—not that elves usually mingled with his kind. They most assuredly never attracted the lycans' notice to such an extent. Perhaps she was a half-breed of some sort.

Cursed hell, Ilar thought.

She was lucky he was old enough to control his primitive urges—or else she would really have something to worry about. If he chose to attack her, there would be no stopping it. She was very fortunate indeed that it was only a group of young soldiers that hunted her.

"C-an yo-u un-derstan-d?" Ilar asked carefully in the old language all races knew. It had been a long time since he'd formed the words and they were stilted with the influence of neglect.

Rhiannon stumbled as the man abruptly released her. Her knees weakened and she fell limp on the ground, too shaken to stand. Her arms wrapped around her chest, trying to draw warmth where there was none. The frigid shoreline mud pressed up into her legs, making it worse. Glancing over her shoulder, she saw that indeed the creatures were gone. She was left alone with her rescuer. She'd have sighed in relief but, as she looked up at the man, all thoughts of safety fled.

Rhiannon froze as curious warmth invaded her limbs. Not only was this man's chest naked, but his legs were bare. Her eyes widened and she couldn't help the insipid look of awe that came to her as she looked over his masculine, hair-roughened calves. He wore only the barest of linen wrapped around his firm waist. His naked feet caught her attention and she wondered if she'd ever seen male feet. He stood as if the uneven stone didn't affect him. His arms hung at his sides, loose. Yet, even in relaxation, they appeared tight and authoritative.

"This dream keeps getting stranger and stranger," Rhiannon said softly, looking him over through the strands of her hair. Her body shivered, her teeth chattered, and she ached in a myriad of ways.

Rhiannon blinked, swallowing nervously as the heat from a blush stained her cheeks. The man placed his hands boldly on his hips. He leaned over to catch her eyes. She should have looked up before that moment. Maybe then she wouldn't have been stunned to find a hard brown gaze close to her face. The man's hair fell forward, parted down the middle, wet and dark brown, and slightly tangled from washing. The straight locks were nearly as long as her waist-length tresses.

For a moment, Rhiannon was sure she was dead— gone straight to a fiery eternity and here was the devil himself to greet her. The dark slash of his brows lowered over his narrowing gaze as he studied her. She shivered anew, her breath ragged.

Her body hurt and she wanted to weep. She was very aware of his inspection of her. She looked down, knowing she must appear dreadful. Seeing her wet gown, stained and ripped beyond repair, she shuddered violently. For a moment, she thought about falling to the stone and waiting for death. Seeing his severe brown gaze, she held back. She wasn't sure she wanted to die by the devil's side.

Only a devil could command the demons that chased her.

Only a devil could make her chilled skin hot by just leaning near her.

Only a devil would have such piercing eyes.

Rhiannon trembled, her limbs too weak to do anything else. His was an accent she didn't readily recognize. His deep voice sounded monstrous—low and harsh, rumbling at her. So why was she waiting to hear it again? She'd heard horror stories about the dark heathen barbarians who lived far into the southern deserts. Maybe, he was one of those. Only, this wasn't a desert. She'd been told deserts were nothing but leagues of yellow sand.

Again she glanced over her shoulder to make sure the beasts were gone. They were, but she couldn't relax. This forceful man before her terrified her nearly as much as the beasts. For a moment, she considered taking back to the stream.

"Do you control the *nietens*?" she asked weakly.

Ilar went rigid at the question. *Nieten*. The human word for beast. She was a mortal and she insulted his people with her narrow-minded slander. He hadn't seen a mortal for over three hundred years—not since they closed the gateway between her world and his. A wave of disgust assaulted him. It would seem the humans hadn't changed.

"Why are yo-u here, mor-tal?" he spat, his eyes darkening. The language quickly came back in his anger.

"Mortal?" She lifted her hand to her face, clearing her matted hair from her eyes to better study him.

Ilar wasn't prepared for her beauty. Even splattered and smeared in mud, she had some of the finest features he'd ever seen. Oh, this was bad. If the lycan guards were excited by her mere scent, they'd boil when they saw her attractiveness. This was very, very bad. He sniffed her again. His body hardened and his resolve weakened. No mortal he'd ever heard of emitted such a potent pheromone on their own. Black magic was at work. But whose? And why?

Ilar frowned. He'd come from bathing in the stream and hadn't been given time to change. If she continued to stare at his midsection in unmaidenly invitation, her mouth working peculiarly, he'd be tempted to provide her with something to stare at. She continued to shiver and he sensed she wasn't about to move.

"Is that what your people call my kind, heathen?" she asked.

Nieten? Heathen? Ilar thought with disgust. He was tempted to teach this little human a lesson in manners.

He wondered what he should do with her. He didn't want to take her home with him, but he was afraid he might not have a choice. He couldn't very well leave her in the forest for the men to fight over.

"You are from the Holy Land?" She looked up at him when he didn't move to speak.

"I am no-t," he answered, not completely understanding what she meant by her question.

"I think I have died," she said, truthfully. There was no other explanation for it. "I think you must be the devil."

At that, Ilar grinned, a slow curling expression that claimed his face—though it wasn't pleasure that radiated there. Feeling the restlessness amongst the lycan who lingered in the forest, he knew he had to get her out of the open air. Her scent was drifting downwind and the others were again picking up her trail. The mind link screamed with their discontent, echoing faintly in his head. If they came back, he wouldn't wish to fight them all.

"That," he stated gruffly, watching her shake in fear of him. He leaned to grab her arm and hauled her back to her feet. "Is the first thing yo-u have said that makes any sense."

Cupid fumed from his perch on the tree, watching Ilar with the woman. Why wasn't he trying to mate with her? Was the human too ugly for even troll magic? No, that was impossible. Such old love magic made men blind to such things and all Ilar was supposed to see was his lust as it consumed him in madness.

The lycan guards had been willing to fight to the death over her. Cupid had been giddy with excitement to see them come running from the bathing pool to track her down. When she cupped the water to her face, she must have sent her scent downstream to the bathing lycans. It all went according to plan—well at least until Lord Ilar showed himself. Too bad the Commander sent the lycans off. He'd been enjoying the show.

Cupid absently stuck a finger up his nose and dug about in the depths. Without stopping to think, he pushed the same finger into his tiny ear and poked it around. As he watched, Ilar pulled the woman up before him. When the bold lycan Commander roughly led the mortal away, Cupid's happy grin widened. Maybe the philter worked after all. It looked as if Lord Ilar was going to take the ugly human home.

Lightheaded with excitement, the troll hopped up and down, forgetting he perched high up on a tree branch. With a grunt of surprise, he fell back and tumbled to the forest floor.

5

Rhiannon gasped as the devilish man jerked her to her feet. Her knees gave when she tried to stand, and she dipped down and he pulled her harder. He didn't give her time to collect herself before brusquely forcing her to walk beside him. Was he angry with her? If so, for what reason? She couldn't tell by his blank expression.

The grip tightened on her arm and he walked faster, leading her along the shoreline. Everything passed by, surreal and dreamlike. The trees were unchanging along the trail, more of the same odd red. The stream bent and curved in the ground.

"Where are we going?" Her voice was frail, breathless.

The handsome, half-naked stranger didn't readily

answer and, when the words finally came, they were abrasive. "I am taking yo-u from the forest. It is not safe for yo-u here."

"I want to go home," Rhiannon told him, again tripping on her own feet as she tried to keep up. The rocks poked at her soles and it was hard to walk with sharp jabs digging into her flesh. She glanced at his bare feet. He didn't seem to have the same problem. "I'm sure my father will reward you greatly for your kindness, Sir Knight, in returning me."

Rhiannon did her best not to stare at the man's naked body wrapped indecently in the cloth. She saw his butt moving beneath the thin material, mesmerizing her and making her weak in a strange, new way. Below his sculpted navel, a thick protrusion moved with his body as he walked. She wondered at it, finally concluding it must be a knife.

Her eyes burned where the dirt still gritted beneath her eyelids and it was getting harder to keep them open. The hand on her flexed, pulling her along as if she were a feather. Her attention was drawn to his grip. The man's bicep was lean muscle—not too large and definitely not too small—as was the rest of him. His ease and power frightened her.

"Please, may I go home now?" she begged softly, worn from her strange ordeal. She tried to free her arm from his grasp, but he didn't let her go. Rhiannon wasn't sure how much farther she could walk. She'd never wanted to collapse upon the ground so badly in her life.

Ilar studied the woman from the corner of his eye, as he dragged her alongside him. He gripped her slender arm, his hand like a manacle. She tripped, trying to keep up with his longer stride. The lycan guards were circling closer, coming back to see her. Gritting his teeth, he frowned as a waft of her potently erotic scent hit him full force. It would seem the magical enticement on her only increased with time. This was serious.

"Please," she begged.

At the feeble plea, he finally stopped to look at her.

Ilar frowned at her deceiving nature. Her wide eyes looked up at him with innocence. He doubted she was innocent. She was human, after all. Humans had tried to hunt his kind into extinction and all because of a few rogue wolves who'd developed a taste for human blood. The rest of them had been peaceful, hunting wild animals in the forest like their natural ancestors and only attacking humans when first provoked. It had been a bloody battle and Ilar had lost many friends. It wasn't something he wanted to relive.

In the end, it was decided the realms should be forever separated. The lycans weren't the only ones to leave the world of mortals. The vampires, who were also hunted because of their 'unnatural' ways, had come with them as did all things of magic—elves, fairies, even the goblins and trolls. They left the realm of humans, tired of being trapped and forced to use magic for mankind's gain. Then it was believed that humans would kill themselves off. It wasn't to be so. To everyone's amazement, the humans thrived.

Ilar knew a few portals between the realms remained. But, until now, no human had ever found a way to cross over them. From what he understood, it should have been impossible. The doors on the mortal side were locked with the strong magic and charms of all immortal races. The only way was for one from the magical realm to go through and bring her back. But to what end? Who would ignore the pact of the covenants that had protected them from human greed for the last three hundred years? There was nothing to be gained by it.

"How did yo-u come to be here?" he asked, unable to stop the question. Her pheromone scent reeled him in, tempting him to step toward her. Ilar had the strangest urge to kiss the muddied she-creature and mate with her like a wild animal. He wondered what she'd do if he ripped the linen from his waist and threw her to the ground. He resisted, disgusted that he could even feel such lust for a human. His breathing became hard, flaring his nostrils as he fought for control.

"I do not know where here is," Rhiannon said.

Ilar's long hair had dried, blowing over his shoulders to reach for her. His gaze narrowed in on her mouth. Her eyes darted back and forth, revealing how nervous she was at his attention, and she again tried to jerk her arm free. He squeezed her harder, stopping when she cried out in pain.

"Mm." He began walking once more, taking a furious pace. He heard the restless howls of the lycans in his brain. They drew closer, unhampered by the thought of their leader's wrath. It was like they were mindless with lust. Sniffing her again, Ilar frowned. He saw why. Her pull was ten times stronger than a cart full of naked lycan females in heat.

He took the long way around to Lycaon, going toward the back entrance of the castle. It wouldn't do to parade this walking enticement through the front gate. If the men of their kind wanted to mate with her, the women of his kind would surely want to kill her. Competition was fierce for they were a fierce people and, with her strange curse, she'd be in for it from both sexes.

Maybe, I should let them kill her and be done with it, he thought.

It was a tempting idea. Even as he considered it, he knew he couldn't.

He was the Commander of the Lycan Guard. It was his duty to discover who sent her and why. If she were killed, he wouldn't get the answers he needed. If the humans had found a way to cross over, they needed to know. It could be disastrous for their realm. And if someone plotted against the lycan, then he needed to know that as well.

Rhiannon tripped behind him in silence. Her bare feet rubbed raw against the rough texture of the forest floor. Twigs and seeds stabbed up into her tender flesh until she was bleeding. The breeze hit her wet gown, making her stiff with cold. Seeing the man's rising anger, she knew better than to complain. She thought of running, but something told her he would catch her. He knew this forest. She didn't. Besides, there were beasts much more frightening looming within the trees.

All of a sudden, the forest changed, growing darker as they came upon a gray wall of uneven stone blocks. It was colder in the shade, causing her to shake violently. Ilar stopped, letting her go. She fell into the wall, her face near a trail of vines that grew over the crevices, sprouting little blue flowers over the surface.

Rhiannon gripped the wall to hold herself up. Her lids dipped over her eyes. She ripped absently at the vines seeking support. Her feet pulsated and her head felt strange as if a swelling grew from the back of it. Gingerly, she felt into her muddied locks. She found a bump the size of a robin's egg and flinched as she pressed into it.

She tried to focus on the peculiar man. "Who are you?"

Ilar felt along the wall. Fitting his finger into a notch, he murmured an incantation and waited as the wall parted to let him through. She gasped as the stone melted apart like liquid and stumbled away from him, eyeing him and then the wall warily. She wobbled on her feet.

"I thought we already established I was the devil." Ilar smirked. If it had been any other situation, he would have enjoyed putting a bit of fear into her, as he played along with the little 'game' she set before him. The lycan liked to play such games—anything to excite the blood and race the heart. Detecting the slight tensing of her shoulders, and knowing she was going to run from him before she even took a step, he frowned and shot forward to grasp her arm.

Oh she was entertaining all right, but the effect she had on his senses was starting to wear on him. Too bad he didn't have a current lover. He would have liked to slake his unexpected desires, easing the thick pain of his arousal inside a warm sheath. He looked the muddy temptress over, eyeing her slender waist. It would be so easy to take her. She was frail, trembling, and small. He bet her body would fit around him nicely, as he pressed her up against the bailey wall. Her fear called out to the hunter in him, but the man in him held back.

"Come," he ordered, exasperated beyond belief and not liking his fantasy. He pulled her back against his chest, intent on keeping her close.

Rhiannon drew a quick breath, holding it as his touch stung her with its force. She stiffened and a weak moan of surprise left her throat. His warmth soaked along her spine and her chilled skin eagerly drank of his heat. His hair whipped over her, hitting across her neck in silken threads. A dark lock caught between her panting lips. A shockwave of pleasure coursed throughout her at his nearness. She welcomed the light-headed feeling.

"Stay by my side and try not to draw notice." His gruff voice pulled her back to reality. By his tone, Rhiannon got the impression he didn't think such a thing was possible. He thrust her to his side, looking her over with a sigh of disgust.

He stepped through the opening in the wall. She tried to pull away from him, apprehensively eyeing the doorway. He grumbled in annoyance, yanking her through it. She called out in loud surprise.

At the sound of her voice, the inhabitants turned to stare at them. Rhiannon stared back. She was glad her hair fell into her face because it hid her fear from view.

They stood in a bailey yard before an enormous castle. The battlements circled the bailey, disappearing in the distance. Square turrets were built in intervals along the outer face, standing tall as lookout towers. A stone house encased the gated entrance. The gate was up so people could walk through it freely. The place was grand, like no other she'd ever seen. Whoever ruled here was indeed very powerful. The wall grew shut behind her and she jolted in alarm, letting loose a high-pitched squeak.

"Yo-u call that not drawing notice?" Ilar grunted in displeasure. He was all too aware of the strange light falling over the men's eyes as they looked at the mortal. He detected her fear and knew the natural hunter inside his fellow lycan would be stirred to greater degrees.

Thankfully, they were in the outer yard by the side gate where only a few of the guard stood watch. The men inquisitively eyed his almost naked state. Their nostrils flared, catching the woman's scent, knowing he hadn't taken her as his lover. Until she was claimed, she was open territory. Their eyes lit in instant battle, ready to fight mindlessly to obtain her.

Rhiannon was unaware of the effect she had on the

men. They all eyed her, the stranger in their midst, with a look akin to hunger. She gazed back, disturbed by them —and not only by their overbold stares. The men were indecently clad in a draping tunic that fell to the top of the knee. The large square pieces were arranged around the shoulders and held in place by a plain brooch. Some didn't have a clasp, just a wrapping of thick material. Arms and one shoulder were left bare, making no mistake that these men could part from their clothing at a moment's notice. Calves were left naked, some cross-strapped with leather bands coming from short boots.

"Are you Scots?" Rhiannon asked, having seen the tartans of the Highlanders. These men's tunics were of a plain color—ranging in earthy tones—and not the plaid patterns of the Scottish clans.

She slowly crept closer to Ilar's side, almost hugging herself to his arm when another of the men slowly smiled at her. It was a hard, wolf-like grin that grew leisurely over his features. His lips parted as if he would pounce atop her frail body and bite into her flesh.

Ilar frowned. A burly guard aggressively stepped forward, as if to make a move for her. He lowered his jaw and silently warned him to back away. The man held rigid, watching the woman closely. Ilar led her past.

"Stay close to my side if you value your life, human," Ilar ordered. Seeing a mated lycan, he telepathically urged him after his clothes by the stream. The man nodded, unaffected by the enchanted woman, and took off to do as he was bid. Ilar knew there was no point in trying to break through to the others with the woman so close at hand. They were beyond reason and the mind link was blocked because of it.

He glanced down at his arm where she gripped him. She kneaded her fingers along his muscles, digging in with her short fingernails. He swallowed, feeling her soft breasts press into him from beneath the wet gown. Her nipples were hard, and it drove him mad. They called to him. Making a fist, he fought the urge to grab her breasts. Her heart raced and his leapt to join the rhythm. She trembled and, all of a sudden, he realized her face was an unnatural pale blue behind the strands of her hair.

Leading her through an entry into the inner bailey yard, Ilar moved straight to the front door of the castle. Rhiannon didn't make a sound. She didn't have to. The people of Lycaon Castle sensed her immediately. The men's thoughts shot with a passionate uproar and the unmated women surged with jealous hatred. Seeing that a brawl was about to start, Ilar turned and swiftly lifted the woman into his protective embrace.

Rhiannon was surprised when the man picked her up, but she didn't protest as she burrowed resignedly into his chest. She was too tired and too sore to complain. Her flesh eagerly soaked in the warmth from his body, racking with shivers once more as she tried to steal his heat.

His muscles moved against her, almost hypnotic. Her fingers wound into his hair, resting near the beat of his heart. She burrowed into his chest. There was something both safe and dangerous in his hold. He smelled fresh, like the stream, like nature. She closed her eyes.

Ilar hastened his steps, rushing her inside the protection of the castle. Her breath fanned over him, sending little trails of longing throughout his tightening form. He passed the main hall where more turned to give the woman curious stares.

Taking the side steps two at a time, he brought her to his personal tower. He would rather put her below in the prisons, far away from him, but he couldn't risk trapping her with an unmated guard and he wouldn't have the other prisoners uprising to get to her.

Usually none would dare to cross his threshold without his summons. But, being as there was black magic afoot, he couldn't afford to take chances. Until he had an opportunity to figure out what was going on, he'd have to keep her safely locked away. Even now, the men in the hall were riled and on the brink of combat for their right to claim the human. If he weren't careful, the whole Lycan Guard would kill each other off.

Her body flopped in his arms, as he took her through

the halls covered with tapestries. The faces of his people stared back at him. Their stitched deeds were a constant reminder of his duty, his heritage, his honor. He steeled himself as he carried her to his bedchamber. There was no time to prepare a guest chamber and there wasn't one already made up. He rarely received guests in his tower —aside from Malak, his lifelong friend, who never complained about the lack of refined comforts his guest chambers had to offer. There were a bed and fireplace, which suited Malak just fine.

Besides, Ilar wanted to keep this woman close. He told himself it was to protect her. But, as he pulled her body into his chest and she didn't protest his hold, he wasn't so sure. His body lurched with intentions. His heart raced, pouring passion into his blood, forcing it into every limb, most notably the limb between his thighs.

Closing the bedchamber door with his foot, Ilar lowered the woman to her feet. She hadn't spoken through the journey upstairs and, come to think of it, she hadn't moved. Frowning, he tilted his head to study her face. Her eyes were closed. Listening to her heartbeat, he heard its faint and even rhythm in his ears. Her breath rasped slightly in her chest, shallow and panting.

Ilar laid her on his bed, scowling as he looked her over. Her features were pale, her lips tinged with blue. She didn't move.

"Mor-tal," he demanded harshly, to see if she would stir.

A low fire burned in the fireplace and he crossed over to throw more logs on the flames until it roared to life. Without thought, he stripped the linen from his waist. Then, going to her, completely naked, he began peeling and ripping the wet layers of her clothing with supernatural speed. He tried to ignore the pleasing flesh he revealed. But his eyes took their own greedy pleasure as his hands dutifully worked. Her small breasts were freed first, the perfect size to fit into his opened mouth. The nipples were hard, begging to be suckled and licked. Her waist was narrow, spanning the width of his spread hand. A thatch of dark blonde curls guarded her opening from him. His body jerked, wanting to conquer.

He crawled next to her on the large mattress and cradled her in his arms. Pulling her tight, he settled her back against his front, liking the feel of her. She shivered violently against his hold but didn't fight him as he warmed her.

Ilar frowned. He'd forgotten that about mortals. They weren't built to withstand the weather like the lycans. Whereas he thought nothing of bathing in the freezing stream, human bodies were frail to such things as extreme cold. He wondered why she hadn't complained. If she had said she was growing ill, he would have helped her. At least, he liked to think he would have.

Ilar cradled her to his naked chest, letting her head rest on a bent arm. Absently, he rubbed his hand along her arms, wrapping his thigh over her slender legs. He was all too aware of the feel of her soft skin beneath his. Her butt was flush to his erection, which found itself pressed tight against two cheeks. Growling, he again cursed the fact he had no lover to slake his desires with.

He would have to get this spell broken soon if he was to have a moment's peace. The keep was in a state of unrest by her brief presence. His men were poised to battle. The women were poised to murder. Even now he heard their discontent knocking at his brain. Not for a second did he believe their attraction to this human female was anything but an enchantment.

He continued to stroke her arms, running his hands up and down. By small degrees she heated to him. Her shivering stopped to all but a few, small, occasional shudders. Her hips stirred, bumping along his thick arousal—an arousal that had been there since catching her at the stream. His touch turned from medicinal to exploring, as he slipped his hand beneath her arm to her hip. He pulled his fingers over her, moving to cup a breast in his palm. His hips jerked, forcing his shaft to rub along her backside. It would be so easy to angle her body, to draw her leg back over his, to sheathe himself inside her wetness. With little movements, he could take her like this, thrusting in from behind.

Ilar grew bolder, moving to massage her other breast. A soft moan, so light and feminine, left her lips, encouraging him. Ilar tensed. His eyes flashed with a dark, possessive excitement. She moaned again, this time louder as her naked back wiggled into his hard heat.

Maybe he'd flip her on her stomach, lifting her hips so he could ride her. Yes, he liked that idea better. Ilar licked his lips. In that position, he'd be able to plunge his shaft deep.

Her head tilted back on her shoulders, moving so he saw her closed eyes and dirty face. He was too aroused to care that she needed a bath. The way she moved, wiggling her butt along his shaft, could only mean she wanted him too. He smelled her longing, her woman's fragrance. Her lips parted in breath as if she beckoned him with a kiss.

The spell over her spread into Ilar's body, potent and hot as it flamed in his blood. He was all too aware of the feel of her. Her legs moved restlessly beneath his thigh. Ilar swallowed, breathing heavily. She was so small, delicate. It would be so easy to turn her and part her thighs to him. Her soft skin caressed him like silk. She moaned again and he couldn't deny her parted lips.

Ilar didn't think as he lowered his mouth to touch hers. His kiss was gentle, testing her, slowly discovering her. He moved her over onto her back, no longer intent on giving warmth as he sought to stir her body to his. He groaned in delight. Her flesh was so frail, so malleable against his harder length. He didn't remember humans being so supple and fragile. Her blood was there, beneath the surface, like tiny rivers dancing beneath the flesh. It had been a long time since he'd felt such softness or such longing. Most lycan women were as hard as the men, toned from their time spent in wolfen form. But this woman was soft, like a fairy or elf, and as delicately featured as a wood nymph only twice as beautiful.

"So warm," Rhiannon mumbled sleepily, her mind dazed to everything but the comfort of the bed beneath her and the hard warmth at her side. She felt as if she could sleep for an eternity.

Rhiannon gasped for breath as a wet probing thrust between her lips, but she didn't move to wake up. She welcomed the inviting warmth inside her mouth, liking the protective embrace of whoever held her. She ached, her breasts tormenting her with pleasure and need as someone pressed against them. The touch was firm yet gentle, so unyielding yet tender. A moan sounded in her head, but she couldn't whisper it past her lips. Whoever was there still kissed her, deepening, exploring, cutting off her weak voice.

Ilar groaned, becoming emboldened. Tempted to investigate their differences further, he glided his hand over her smooth hip, lifting a leg to the side. He drew his mouth away and looked down over her flat stomach to her slit. He smelled the start of her desire. It called his lips down to the apex of her thighs. He detected the glistening invitation of moisture as it gathered in readiness for him along her folds.

As he reminded himself that this female was a human, he hesitated only slightly. He couldn't stop. Human or not, she felt too good. It had been too long since he'd satisfied his baser needs and they now called to him in protest of that neglect.

Drawing a finger over her hip, he followed the natural crease in her leg, down to her most sensitive of flesh. She shuddered as he neared her wet center. His eyes rolled back, having seen too much as he watched his hand explore. As he found the small thatch of her hair with his fingers, he groaned and again kissed her.

She mumbled something into his lips, but the blood roaring through his tight body kept him oblivious to her words. Ilar traced her mouth with his tongue, hungry for more, even as he drew out his discovery. Soon his finger mimicked the movements of his tongue, parting her silken lips, testing their moist response as he circled over her opening. She was wet, ready, hot. His thumb circled over the tight nub, causing a weak sound to escape her.

Ilar grew bolder, rolling so that he came above her. His mouth trailed over her dirty skin, not noticing the mud as he brushed kisses along her throat, her jutting collarbone. His legs intertwined with hers and he molded his body against her length. His knees instinctively parted her thighs, pushing her open until she awaited him, widespread. He rocked his shaft against, rubbing naturally back and forth along her slick folds, preparing to enter.

Ilar rubbed his chest against her small breasts, keeping the tips budded with the heat from his skin. His elbow braced his weight as he explored the sweeping curve of her hip. She whimpered softly in what his mind could only take as approval and encouragement.

Lightly, he cupped a breast in his palm, kneading as he held it for his lips. The globe was so soft, delicate. It drove him mad. He licked a nipple, groaning with passion at the feel of it against his tongue. It puckered for him, reaching for more.

Ilar became more insistent. He didn't think to slow. His hips rose as he slipped himself along her wet slit, rubbing his hot erection against her, pushing along her opening. All he felt was his passion, his hunger, his desperate need to possess her. He prepared to thrust mindlessly into her depths. Surely a woman who made such whimpering noises knew what she wanted.

Rhiannon's eyes opened in confusion as she felt a hot, wet stroke along her chest. The same madness was between her thighs. For a moment, she couldn't think. It was strange but felt so good. She wanted more.

Her eyes darted around in her head, wondering what could be wreaking such havoc on her body. With a jolt of surprise, she felt the brush of hair tickling her sides. Looking down her body, she saw a dark head affixed to her naked breast. Desire was instantly replaced by shock, as she jolted to full awareness.

"*Ah,*" she cried. She kicked her legs, trying to close her knees, as she fought the large body atop hers. At her movement, the hardness between her thighs pressed in. The pleasure she felt at the intimate contact scared her more than the shock of it.

Ilar felt her buck against him. The action caused her opening to dip onto his arousal, swallowing the smooth head of his shaft into her wondrously tight depths. Just that small taste of her wet passage felt better than he'd imagined it would. He groaned in delight and didn't immediately clue in that she fought to get him off. But, then, he heard her cry out.

"Help." Rhiannon hollered, her voice hoarse. She

struck him desperately with her fists, hitting his head, his back, anything she could reach. The feeling stirring inside her did strange things to her head. Her body wanted more, even as her mind fought the pleasure.

Rhiannon screamed. Whatever it was that burned and pressed into her opening became bolder. The heat probed her, moving deeper. She pulled her hips back, terrified, as she was sure she was to be impaled by the thick weapon, possibly killed. And yet, the feelings it caused felt like sweet, torturous death and an insane part of her cried to let her body die. Fear was easier to accept at the moment and she embraced it, yelling, "Get off me, you... *wyrm*. Help. Someone, please, help me!"

Ilar pulled back, retreating from of her completely. He was confused, bewildered, in pain. His chest heaved with unspent desire, as his shaft throbbed in protest. He'd been so close to slipping fully inside her tight body. Even now the proof from her body dried on him. She'd been ready, willing. Hadn't she?

No woman had ever denied him entrance. No woman had ever stopped him. In fact, it was usually he who turned the females away. He blinked, trying to work his way from the fog in his brain. Her blue eyes stared at him in accusation. Even angry and flushed, she looked beautiful. He wanted her, needed her. But, Ilar had never taken an unwilling woman to his bed, had never had an unwilling woman *in* his bed. That he'd been about to do that very thing amazed him.

Rhiannon scurried back on the mattress, folding her naked body into a protective ball. She was hot, too hot, nearly dizzy. Her thighs throbbed and ached, remembering the strange fullness of him next to them, wanting it back so badly that her stomach twitched.

"What did you do to me?" she demanded, hoarse, scared. Her gaze journeyed over his naked form. He didn't even try to hide from her. He was a large man to be sure if the haloing of light from the fireplace gave any indication. His body was shadowed, but she could make out the vague protrusion of his shaft pointing in her general direction as if it called forward the attack. Though it was a weapon, she'd been a fool to think it a blade he wore beneath his linen.

Closing her eyes to him, Rhiannon hugged her legs tighter. Her body churned uncontrollably, alive with heated sensations. Her stomach lurched.

"I kept you alive," Ilar said, enraged by her rejection of him. The human words came back to him with greater and greater ease until his stunted effect on them had almost faded. His mind cleared by small degrees. He realized that, as he touched her, she hadn't been touching him back, at least not in full passion. She'd been lying unconscious, only moaning lightly. His anger turned in on himself. His words not as strong as before, he said, "I was warming you. The water from the stream…"

"I don't need you to warm me," she denied, shaken. As she sensed the danger to be somewhat past, she relaxed her death grip on her body. An eye opened to look at him. Seeing he was still unclad, it quickly closed. "The fire will do fine."

At that he grunted.

Rhiannon blinked to hear him move and looked fully at him. Crossing over to a trunk, he pulled it open and grabbed a tunic. His naked butt flexed without an ounce of fat. A slight dimple was carved into the side of the firm cheek. His flesh was bronzed all over, kissed by sunlight. The man was wickedly alluring to her senses. When he leaned over, her body jerked in sudden enjoyment at the sight. She wanted to touch him, draw him against her. Her slit throbbed to have him back, rubbing and probing with his heat.

Rhiannon saw two soft globes dipping beneath his larger weapon. Her mouth went dry. She wasn't a fool. She knew men were shaped differently, had heard talk of it, but never had she thought she'd be so intrigued to see it. Shamed, she looked away, knowing she shouldn't be staring.

Rhiannon, becoming all too aware of her vulnerable state, pulled a thick wool coverlet over her body to hide it from view. She was glad this powerful man had called off his attack. She was positive he'd been about to injure her with what he was about. Her lower body trembled. She was still able to feel the stretching violation. Oddly, she still wasn't as repulsed by it as she should have been—even with her sanity returning.

"Where are my clothes?" she inquired weakly, breathless, near fainting.

Ilar draped a red tunic around his body with a practiced swing of the arms. Within seconds, he had a circular brooch secured at the shoulder. The clothing didn't help. It hid his butt, but she could still see his strong side, his muscular arms, broad shoulders. Nodding toward the floor, he drew her attention to the muddied, wet gown.

"I will find you something more appropriate," he said. Eyeing her dirty frame, he frowned and wrinkled his nose in what looked like disgust. "I will also find you a bath."

Rhiannon nodded, too grateful for his hospitality to berate him further. Biting the inside of her lip, she asked, "Where are we?"

"You are in the realm of all things magical." Ilar scowled as he realized she hadn't known. Silently, he cursed, *By all that is sacred. This is a wicked mess.*

Her confusion would make his job a great deal

harder. Ilar had a feeling the quicker he could solve this mystery, the better it would be for his kind. He had every intention of finding whoever brought her through the portals and forcing them to take the wench back.

"Magic?" Rhiannon gasped weakly, before laughing. "No, it isn't possible."

He arched a brow and did nothing to convince her.

He's way too handsome for his own good, Rhiannon thought. Unbidden, the feel of his mouth came back to her breast and her skin jumped at the memory. His eyes narrowed as if he knew her thoughts. She swallowed, mortified to be thinking them. What was wrong with her? She didn't want a man, any man. She wanted freedom, freedom to run about her father's keep.

"Say I believe you," she said, trying to bring their thoughts back to the problem at hand. "Why did you bring me here? What is it you want?"

"I did not bring you," he answered. He put his hands on his hips, drawing her eyes to the slight bulge that still stood beneath the material of his tunic. "Nor did I invite you. Your kind is not welcomed here, mor-tal."

"My kind?" Eyeing him cautiously, she wasn't sure she wanted her next questions answered. "Why do you keep speaking as if we're different? What are you? Where have you taken me? What is this place?"

Ilar smiled, coming up with an idea. Maybe if she

looked at him with complete fear, he'd be able to tamp back his sexual craving for her, though the bloodlust would only serve to stir the hunter in him. It couldn't hurt to try, though the way his body pulsated with need, he doubted anything would tame the sizzling lust. Ilar could well control the hunter. It was the man he was having a hard time reining in.

With that in mind, he stalked toward her. A deadly expression settled on his face. He crawled on all fours onto the bed. When he was close to her, nearly coming above her slender body, he looked deeply into her eyes.

"I'm Lord Ilar, Commander of the Lycans," he said with a rumble that left her feeling faint and extremely fragile. "And you, my dear mor-tal, have entered into the den of the man-beast."

Ilar didn't care for the term *man-beast*, but it was one her kind would recognize.

Rhiannon barely heard his words before his gaze filled with liquid gold, slivering until the color overtook his eyes. His face elongated slightly, growing with fine dark hair. His mouth parted to show dangerously long, sharp teeth. Ilar didn't shift completely, but only enough so she got his meaning. It didn't take long for him to receive the scream he expected.

Rhiannon yelled at the top of her lungs, violently pulling back from him. This creature is what had touched her so intimately? Those teeth had latched onto her breast? With a gasp, she fell off the side of the bed, landing on her tailbone in a bruising smack against the stone. Her scream turned into a groan of pain, but she didn't stop as she crawled backward, dragging the wool coverlet with her. Only stopping as the stone of the wall blocked her retreat, she froze, huddled as far from him as she could get. Her hand swept against the stone, looking for a weapon that was not there.

"You cannot exist," she said in denial, clutching the wool to her chest. But the truth was right there before her. It all added up—the *nietens* at the stream, the magical opening in the wall, the frightening voice in her tower bedchamber before she blacked out—how could she have forgotten that until now? Then, seeing his eyes, still shining with golden threat, she shivered. It was as he said. She was somehow in a world of magic. "This place cannot be real. It is not... possible. I must be mad. I've gone insane."

"Do you need me to demonstrate how real I can be?" he charged, standing from the bed to tower over her from the side. He lifted his hand to his shoulder and part of him hoped she'd say yes. She didn't. Instead, she shook her head in furious denial.

"No, I believe you."

"Good." He dropped his hand and let his face shift

back to man, only keeping his eyes the same golden hue. "Believe this, mortal. I'm your master so long as you are here. If you even dare to disobey me, I will punish you. You will not leave this tower without my permission. Mark me, I will find who brought you here and I will discover why."

"I'm not afraid of you," she blustered, refusing to be such a coward. She rediscovered her backbone at his arrogant tone. What had happened to her that she'd turned into such a weakling? Sitting taller, she didn't get up from the floor. "I'm not afraid of your punishments, *nieten*. I do not recognize you as my master."

At that Ilar chuckled, very aroused by her outburst. Letting his eyes darken back to a devilish brown, he said enigmatically, "You should be frightened, mortal. Though I find much amusement in your show of strength, it does not change things."

"What are you going to do? Beat me?" she spat. "I have no fear of death or pain. Say what you will, but I will not cower before you."

"It would be more convincing if you were not huddled on the floor," he informed her.

She tried to stand but ended up staring at him.

"Who said anything about my punishment being one of pain?" He stepped toward her, knowing the moment his meaning sunk in.

Rhiannon's eyes widened. Her mouth gaped, and she recoiled. "You would dare to ravish me? But it won't work. You are a... a beast. We cannot possibly—oh."

His low chuckle stopped her words. The look in his eyes said that their coupling most definitely could work. To her shame, she remembered that it had been working. He pursed his lips together, clucking in disapproval of her words. In a tone so wickedly soft, he said, "When I take you it will not be rape, mortal. I will touch you in ways that will bend you to my resolve. You will crawl around on your knees for me. You will long for me, beg for me. You will beg to have this beast inside you. You will publicly be branded as my lover."

"You mean your whore." The fire had dried his hair straight, and she had the strangest urge to touch the flowing locks, wrapping them around her wrists as a way to control him. "I'll never submit to you in such a way, *nieten*. Send me home. I have no wish to be here. My presence can be of no advantage to you. Send me home or I will make you sorry."

"Do not raise challenges you do not wish met," he warned. "Unlike you, mortal, we lycans thrive on challenge."

"Quit calling me mortal, beast. My name is Lady Rhiannon of Weilshire. You will treat me according to my station."

"You have no power here, mortal," he dismissed her claim. "Nor does your human ranking matter. You would do very well to remember that in the future."

Rhiannon grumbled under her breath. He was right, of course. She didn't have any power in this strange place and she was far too weak from her ordeal to come up with a proper plan of action. She had to think. She had to be smart. Yelling at the man-beast wasn't very smart.

Ilar saw her head drop slightly. The battle was over for now and he wanted nothing more than to get far away from her tempting presence. Already his body sought a release he couldn't claim. He might threaten, but he couldn't mate with her without careful consideration of the consequences. Once the news of her presence got out, he'd have a lot of explaining to do. He only hoped he could come up with the right answers.

Ilar leaned over to grab a pair of his boots. Without a backward glance, he left her cowering alone in the bedchamber. Cursing bitterly, he slammed the door and locked it resolutely behind him.

6

"WHAT IS THIS INFERNAL RACKET?" KING LARUS yelled, glaring past the giant circular pit of flames that lit the council hall. He sat atop a long stone table, rubbing wearily at his temples. His eyes bore into Lord Ilar. Slowly, he lowered his arm to lie along his crossed legs.

Ilar's mouth pulled up at the side. He knew that the elected king sometimes chose to hide out in the council hall when he had a lot on his mind. The hall was dead silent. They were the only two in the room. What Larus referred to was the restlessness searing through their brains. The mind link was now overflowing with discontent. Through the growling, he'd heard the king's faint call to him.

"You haven't smelled her?" Ilar inquired, wryly, answering in the more comfortable fit of their shared language. His body still churned with the aftereffects of his encounter with the delectably soft—*ugh*—with the infuriating mortal.

"Smelled...?" Larus began, only to scowl. He gave a dark look, furrowing his brows, as he roared, "Is that what this is about? A female? I will have the entire guard hanged by their front paws for this nonsense. No female could be worth such insanity. I don't care if she's in heat and dripping pheromone."

Ilar nodded, unable to help his grin. His mind turned to the mud-covered maiden in his bedchamber. Even now when he was away from her, he felt her lingering temptation. He had half a mind to join in the others' howling. He held firm, staying quiet.

"Where is she now?" Larus grumbled. "Naked, out on the exercise field, doing a dance of seduction?"

"No, she's locked safely away in my bedchamber," Ilar answered.

"You don't say?" The king smiled roguishly. "You've claimed her then? Did my call bring you away from her? Pray tell, if that is the case, I will gladly send you to finish your task."

"No," Ilar answered, his grin fading. He remembered all too well the feel of her soft body and the sweet taste of her breast, the slick, hot feel of her... oh, this was bad. He forced a deep breath. He also recalled her fear of him.

Larus saw the Commander's look and chuckled. Ilar continued, "I thought it better than anywhere else. At least there she's locked away from causing mischief."

A particularly loud howling sounded, making them both flinch. This was getting to be too much. The mind link was customarily reserved for communicating in lycan form, not laying thought to sexual frustration and obsession.

"Ah, curse it all." Larus snarled. His lean body leapt up from the table and he landed gracefully on his feet. His draping green tunic and cloak ruffled slightly as he moved. The gold embroidery around the edges weighed down the ends. "They break the mind link with this unrest. I won't stand to have our communication disrupted. What if there was an emergency? All our lives would be put in danger. I called to you nigh fifteen minutes before you answered."

Ilar turned to follow Larus as he moved to go through the side door. They came to a long empty stone passageway that would take them toward the weapons' chamber. Torches burned in sconces along the wall, casting eerie shadows. The king was right, of course. Ilar had thought of the same thing.

Larus's lighter features lifted slightly with a small grin. Clapping his friend on the back, he stated, "It has been a while since you had a lover, Ilar. Do us all a kindness and bind her to you. I would consider it a royal favor if you put an end to this noise. Once I can again think, we will further discuss this matter. I relieve you of your duty until this particular obligation is done."

"I don't think it's wise for me to claim her. She—" Ilar began.

"Ah," Larus laughed. "You can't tell me you don't want her. She must be a true find if she has the whole Lycan Guard on edge. Pray, put us out of our misery before I have a chance to smell her. Or order one of your men to do the deed. I care not, just—"

"She's human," Ilar stated bluntly. His eyes narrowed.

Larus skidded to a stop and for a long moment did not move. His face fell, all traces of amusement gone. "Human? Impossible. She cannot be a full blood." He turned to study his friend. "You're positive? She's not an elfling-human half breed from the old days? Did you not mistake her scent? It has been a long time since any of us have smelled the mortals."

"I'm sure. She's mortal. Full blooded." Ilar frowned, sharing a humorless look with the king. His eyes glittered gold. He quietly told him everything that had happened, leaving out the body-warming. "I believe someone has placed a curse upon her, making her irresistible to our kind. You should have seen the way the men fought over her when I found her near the bathing pool. Toa and Fal were ready to battle to the death to claim her. When I walked her inside, I was afraid I'd have to crush their skulls to keep them at bay. Whatever her reason for being here, it isn't good."

"You are right, of course, Commander. This isn't a good sign. It means one has dared to open the portals to the human world," Larus said softly. "Do you think the vampires would be so bold?"

"I have thought of them," Ilar admitted. There was no love lost between the vampire clans and the lycans. "But there is no proof. I don't think they would be so challenging of the race covenant."

"Does this human have a name?" Larus asked, thoughtful.

"Lady Rhiannon of Weilshire," Ilar answered, getting the cheerless curse he expected.

"It had to be a human noble," Larus said. His dark eyes narrowed in deep thought, sparkling with gold. "Why couldn't it have been a peasant? If I remember correctly, the humans put more stock into the lives of their nobles. I don't suppose that has changed in the last three hundred years."

"I'd have great cause to think the mortals are very much the same." Ilar frowned. "She seemed to believe her title would give her privilege."

"Is her family one of great power? Is this something we need to be concerned about?"

"Beyond her own self-importance, I cannot tell you."

"You must discover where she came from and why, before the other races blame us for her presence." Larus sighed heavily. "Whoever did this could have known our mind link would be disrupted. I'll close the gates and put the castle on alert until this is resolved. I'll also speak to the men. Hopefully, when they know what is happening, they will be able to resist her siren's pull. I'm sorry, my friend, but I leave her under your guard. She is your first responsibility. See that she stays out of trouble. Until we know why she's here, we cannot let harm befall her."

Ilar nodded. He had feared that would be the case.

"Let us hope the effects of the spell will wear off once she has been locked away for a while," Larus said, again scowling as loud grunts sounded in his brain.

With concentration they could quiet the noise, but it took a lot of energy to block it entirely. It was energy the busy king couldn't afford to expend. Not to mention that doing so was dangerous. If there were a call to arms, they would need to hear it. They would have to live with the noise for now.

Ilar grimly nodded. He couldn't ignore a royal decree. Lady Rhiannon, the human, was his responsibility.

7

RHIANNON LET LOOSE A LONG BREATH OF contentment as steam rose over her body. Staying true to his word, Ilar had sent a bath for her. What he forgot to mention was that a horde of little winged fairies would deliver it. She almost fainted when the door unlocked and a bath came flying into the bedchamber, seemingly unattended.

The fairies had buzzed around her head, checking her out, wrinkling their naturally upturned noses in distaste at the wool coverlet she wore for clothes. They all wore beautiful gowns that glistened like stars. She couldn't understand what they said but heard the words 'human' and 'mortal' a few times followed by impertinent giggles and hair pulls.

Rhiannon was again locked inside the tower prison

when the winged creatures left. The chamber wasn't so bad. In fact, it was much better than her previous quarters in her father's tower. She could not miss the irony that she had exchanged one tower prison for another. Only this time her jailer was much more intimidating.

Judging from the trunks of male clothing, she guessed she stayed in Ilar's bedchamber. She wondered where he would spend the night, being as she now had his quarters. His threat of making her his whore still stung. However, after careful reflection, she thought that he tried to scare her into submission. She had been rather irritable with him and he did save her from the man-beasts at the stream.

Even if she was a *mor-tal*, as he so willingly spat, she was a noblewoman. Surely even this race, with their comforts so close to her own, would respect the position of a lady. If she did not dwell too long on the fact that she was in a magical world, in a place priests warned about, she could begin to think logically about her predicament. Besides, the whole coming together probably wouldn't work being as they were obviously made so differently.

"It is not so hard to believe that I have come to a land of magic," she said to herself. "I have known of its existence all my life. It is no more improbable than being taken prisoner by the Scots."

Perhaps after the layer of mud was cleansed from her

skin and hair, he'd be better able to see her true ranking. Rhiannon smiled at the thought. Yes, once he was convinced, she was indeed a noblewoman, he would be honor bound to take her back home. It was a simple enough plan. She had never been accused of being anything but a lady.

As the hot bath water soaked into her weary bones, she stopped to look around. The flames in the large fireplace burned brightly, casting the gray walls in a golden light. Her stomach growled, but she ignored it. The room was spacious, doubling as a sort of bower. Beautifully carved high-backed chairs with plush cushioned seats were near a long-slotted window. Next to the chairs was a carved table of dark wood. Strange rugs lined beneath the window, made from a type of wool. She imagined, being man-wolves, they wouldn't favor using pelts to decorate their chambers.

In the corner there was an old chest. It had a thick iron lock on the front. Curiosity piqued, she bit her lip trying to determine whether or not she could pick the latch. In the end, she decided it would be best not to pillage his belongings.

Rolling back her head, she closed her eyes. Rhiannon wondered if her father knew she was missing yet. She hoped he didn't worry too much. Agrona would undoubtedly be pleased to hear it.

Rhiannon scrunched up her face, wondering if her sister had anything to do with her current situation. Then, deciding Agrona knew even less of the black arts than she did, she dismissed the idea. Agrona may not like her most days, but she would never hurt her.

She didn't need to look behind her to know what the gigantic bed looked like. The fairies had changed the bedding, taking away the covers dirtied by her body. Already its soft depths and rich texture were burned shamefully into her memory. What exactly was Ilar doing to her when she woke up? She was sure there was no need for his lips to be where they were or for his battering ram to be next to her womanly area. Rhiannon was barely able to even think the words. Though, strange as it seemed, the feel of him hadn't been entirely disagreeable.

What was she thinking? It wasn't pleasant to have a stranger, and a *nieten* at that, touch her. It was horrible—horrible and wrong and shameful and wet. Yeah, wet was bad—really, really bad. Wasn't it?

"Oh, Rhian, you are a shameful, wicked, evil, wretched girl." Her words were heated, as she pressed her palm against the offending breast that refused to stop aching. As if her upper body wasn't bad enough with its thoughts and feeling, her lower body wasn't to be outdone. It throbbed and heated in what she could only surmise was a strange excitement.

Reluctantly standing from the warmth of the tub as a self-punishment for her impious thoughts, Rhiannon began the long task of wringing out her waist length hair. Spying what looked like a thick comb on the fireplace mantel, she reached for it, still standing in the filthy water.

The comb had tangles of dark brown hair trapped in the tines. Wrapping an end around her finger, she slowly pulled the strand up for view in the firelight. It drifted, sticking intimately to her breast and stomach, the long, dark trail contrasting her lighter skin. Shivering, Rhiannon shook her head and said to herself, "Wicked, wicked girl."

8

ILAR SHOULD HAVE KNOCKED BEFORE OPENING HIS bedchamber door. He knew it even before he reached for the thick oak. On the other hand, it was his bedchamber. Why should he knock before going into his own chamber?

Scheming did have its privileges.

Ilar grinned as he was rewarded for his lack of propriety with an ample view of his naked prisoner's luscious backside. A glorious abundance of drying blonde curls showered over her shoulders, gliding in sinful tantalization down her narrow back to brush atop her waist. Covered in mud, he hadn't expected her skin to be the color of fresh cream. Nor did he expect it to be so damnably smooth. He instantly wanted to lick her skin, tasting the whole length of it.

Ilar could see firelight glowing golden between her thighs, thighs that were parted ever so naturally. Smelling the perfume of her enchantment, he groaned. His eyes found and held to her backside. His mouth opened, wanting to take a little bite of that adorable, supple, ever so round...

"What do you think you are doing?" Rhiannon screeched. Instantly, she dove for cover behind the bed and crawled over the floor to the far side. "So much for being treated like a lady. Though I suppose I should hardly expect *you* to have manners."

Ilar sighed in loud disappointment. He hadn't been done looking. Even though he had taken care of his needs after leaving her by stroking himself to release, he was again aroused to the point of aching.

"Do all beasts lack manners or just you?" she insisted, angry. Her head popped out from behind the bed as she glared at him. The red color staining her cheeks was more from self-consciousness than anything else.

Ilar's throat went dry. Her blue eyes were wide, soulful. Even in their anger, they had an alluring call to them. Her lips were full—made for kissing. Her nose was straight, proud. Her cheekbones were carved high in her oval face. She reached up to stretch across the bed and grabbed at a gown the fairies had left for her. For a moment, he watched her breasts drag over his bed before she hid once more from view. From where he stood, he could see she tried to dress from her place on the floor.

"This is my bedchamber," he answered belatedly.

"A gentleman would knock first." she fumed, jerking her arms into soft sleeves. "You knew I was here. You ordered the bath."

The green material fitted tightly to her skin, and she struggled as it stuck to her damp body. Truthfully, his possessive look excited her. She'd been staring at the dark strand of his hair when he'd walked in. It adhered to her flesh so she could see what it looked like circling her breast. Reaching beneath her skirt, she found the strand and pulled it off her stomach. Standing once she was decently covered, she jerked her hair off her back to lie over the gown. "You are fortunate that I will not demand to have you reprimanded."

A wolfish grin crept onto his face at her last comment. In a low tone that sent shivers racking her already frail body, he said, "You soon forget, my lady. You have no power here."

"Surely even you can recognize the rules of propriety." She put her hands on her hips. "Or is your land so barbaric you cannot act like a gentleman?"

"Even you, mortal, can recognize that I am your only friend in this barbaric land," he quickly returned.

The dress the fairies had found for her was stunning in its simplicity. It hugged dangerously tight to her curves, outlining her body to the point his imagination had to do little to see it. Good thing it modestly covered her cleavage, or else he wouldn't be able to stop himself from ripping it off her.

Rhiannon frowned. He needed to quit looking at her like that, licking his lips as if she were a pastry. It was doing strange things to her.

"What will it take to negotiate my freedom?" she asked. Fighting with him would get her nowhere. She'd have to remember he was half animal and make allowances for his lack of manners. She was a lady and she would teach this mutt to heel if it were the last thing she ever did. His arrogance was not acceptable.

"You don't have the power to negotiate, nor are you in the position." He strolled past her to sit on one of the high-backed chairs, eyeing her with forced dispassion. "It has been decided that I'm your master until the reason for your presence here is discovered. Do you have anything you would like to tell me to help expedite your departure?"

"I wish you would go to the devil," she snapped, not liking his highhanded tone one bit.

"Do you have anything you would like to tell me about how you came to be here?" he clarified, steepling his fingers lazily under his chin as he studied her. His tone was condescending as if he dealt with an unruly child.

If she had a knife, she'd cut his hair. The overlong length was a distraction. He'd braided the sides back and up to keep them from his devilishly handsome face. Rhiannon's cheeks flamed an angry red.

"If I knew how I got here," she said through clenched teeth, "then I would know how to get home, wouldn't I? And we would not be having this aggravating conversation."

His eyes narrowed in warning at her tone. This interrogation wasn't going as smoothly as he'd hoped.

"For all I know, you kidnapped me," she charged.

"So you were kidnapped," he said. *Now we might be getting somewhere.*

"Obviously," she huffed, rolling her eyes. Her face hardened as she glowered at him.

Or not, he mused.

"And the mud?" Ilar asked. He rubbed his finger along his lower lip. "Are you always that... unclean?"

Her jaw dropped open in affront. He grinned.

"You have to be the rudest... *thing* I have ever met." Her fists found her waist as she stared him down.

Thing? Ilar shot to his feet. It would seem she had no liking for his kind. Her prejudice was like a slap in the face. He could not tolerate these insults. It was time she learned to curb her ignorance in his presence.

Charging forward, he grabbed onto her arms and shook violently. "Do not forget that this *thing* is all that keeps you from harm. Should I decide you are not worthy of my charity, I'll throw you to the wolves, so to speak. Let you fend off their advances. The smell of your fear leaks from you and they will tear you apart before you even take two steps."

Rhiannon's mouth dropped slightly, her eyes rounding in instant horror. Ilar didn't know why, but he was sorry to see it.

"Please, my lord," she said, staring up at him, pleading with her troubled gaze. "Don't do that. I will not forget that it is you who keeps me from the wolves."

Ilar frowned, not liking the effect her soft words had on him. The erotic scent of her curse eased its way into him, tantalizing his senses. His already taut body grew even more so to see her vulnerability.

"I have done nothing wrong." She didn't move to touch him and his hands grew almost tender as he kept hold. She didn't pull away. His magnetic eyes trapped her. "Please, Lord Ilar, I want to go home now. My father will be worried about me. I don't know anything about this. I just woke up, and I was here in your world. Won't it be better for everyone if I left? It's not like anyone from my home would believe me if I said where I had been."

"You cannot be permitted to leave," Ilar said, his tone hard, final. A part of him didn't wish to see her go. He was sure the feeling was the spell's doing. Nevertheless, it felt very real. Softly, he added, "Not until we discover what and who brought you here and why."

Until they knew the nature of her curse, they couldn't risk sending her back. If the spell was strong enough, the others might be tempted to follow her to the mortal realm. Such a thing would be disastrous. It would be their realm's undoing. He wouldn't see more bloodshed. Three hundred years had not been enough to erase the memory of the carnage the last time their two races had battled. He doubted humans would ever be ready to accept the lycans into their midst.

"Please, Ilar," Rhiannon asserted, knowing before the words came out that he wouldn't be swayed on this point. She lifted her hand, lightly letting it rest atop his chest. His heart beat firmly under her palm and she shivered as the soft length of his hair stirred near her fingers.

Drawing her hand back, she swallowed nervously. He was too close to her. His masculine scent affected her reasoning. She looked almost dreamily at his lips and her eyelids dipped slightly.

"Maybe, my coming to be here was a mistake, an

accident," she said. "Maybe it doesn't mean anything is wrong. I don't have the power to do any harm to you. You must see that."

Oh, but she was wrong. Ilar saw the way her eyes melted and dipped with a soft, teasing light. It called to him, beckoned him. He heard the howling in his head, not lessened by distance or time. Already she had wreaked more havoc on his world than he'd seen in a long, long time.

Communication was down between the lycans. The men were at odds, ready to kill each other off to be rid of competition for her hand—brothers, best friends, old men, it didn't matter. Only the mated were unaffected. Unfortunately, mated lycans were rare these days. If she even tried to wield her power over his kind, she would be successful. She could call the entire Lycan Guard to her control and they wouldn't question her. She was more dangerous to his kind than she realized.

Naturally being a creature of potent sexuality, Ilar couldn't resist the pout on her lips nor the look in her lovely eyes. With a groan, he grabbed her. Pulling her to him, he instantly opened his mouth wide, forcing a hot kiss to her mouth.

Rhiannon gasped in surprise at the suddenness of his passion. She hadn't expected it. She shook as his tongue tried to pry her lips apart. His teeth dug into her tender flesh when she didn't readily give him entrance, demanding she open up to him.

A sharp tooth nicked her lip. Ilar groaned in approval as he tasted the blood from the cut. It called his primal nature to the forefront. He sucked her lip between his, sipping the wine of her body. His kiss deepened, consuming, claiming, taking no prisoners, as his hot tongue conquered and massaged every last inch of her mouth.

Rhiannon was frightened. She tried to strike his arm, but it was as if he didn't feel her. His mouth was having a dizzying effect on her head, weakening her will to resist him. He sucked ferociously at her tongue until it slipped into his mouth. Her fist hit lighter and lighter until it stopped altogether. She gripped her fingers into his draping tunic. She couldn't breathe. Her heart thundered, calling out to him.

Ilar's hands were on her back, holding her to his chest. She burned, eager to discover what it was he'd been doing to her body when she awoke with him between her legs. His mouth stole her air until she thought she might pass out. Tentatively, she tried to return his kiss, but his mouth was too much in control to let her take the lead.

Just when she was sure her world would darken from lack of air, his lips let her go. His eyes filled with liquid gold, promising things she didn't understand. His nostrils flared. Unfamiliar sensations swirled in her. She tasted her blood on her lips, salty and strange.

Ilar growled, pressing her back until she hit the wall. He dug his hands at her gown, lifting it, baring her smooth legs to his touch. Drawn to feel her heat, he slipped his fingers between her thighs, rubbing over her mound of hair. She was wet and ready for him. He smelled it, felt it, needed it. He moved to lift the bottom of his draping tunic, his arousal eager to push inside her warm body as his mouth had her lips.

Rhiannon gasped at his forceful ways. He dipped to her neck and, as his lips parted, she saw fangs. Thinking he meant to bite her as he had her lips, she screamed. "Stop. Help!"

Ilar pulled back. Her cry echoed in his head. He wasn't the only one who had heard her plea. The mind link jumped with a feverish rampage as the soldiers grunted and growled in an effort to answer her call. They became furious, screaming in his head, howling viciously, snarling and snapping, threatening him—their Commander—with insults and warnings.

Ilar dropped his hands from her and took a shaky step back. It wasn't enough. He could still smell her, sense her, taste her blood. His loins throbbed, aching, needing, seeking fulfillment, brimming painfully with a desire only her body could sate. This time stroking himself wouldn't be enough. She was in his blood and there was no getting her out. It was beyond obsession. It was beyond reason. Never should a man be made to feel such longing, such burning insanity. He shook his head, nearly storming to the door to get away from her.

His eyes shot golden fire as he turned around to look at her. He was tortured, confused. The howling wouldn't stop. Even now, his body urged him to go and finish his claiming by any means necessary. He moved toward her, only to hold back in an effort of great restraint. Seeing the blood staining her trembling lips, he said hoarsely, "I will have food delivered."

Ilar moved as if to leave, only to pause, taking great breaths of air.

Rhiannon shivered. She wanted to reach for him but kept back. Her limbs felt cold. She didn't understand what happened inside her body when he was near. All she knew was that she wanted the man-beast to continue what he'd been doing before she panicked.

"Ilar?" She finally moved as if to touch his rigid shoulder, eager to draw him back into her arms, eager to feel him as he had her. He was breathing heavily, as if in pain. A shudder moved over his spine at her word. He refused to look at her. His body fascinated her, aroused her curiosity beyond measure.

Curse her feminine outcries anyway.

"No." The gruff sound made her recoil in fear. The beast was in that voice. She backed away from him. Without further comment, he slammed out the door, locking her inside.

Rhiannon felt her wet lips, stained with crimson, swollen from his kisses. She sank wearily to her knees. What was that all about? Was she being punished? If so, it was the best punishment she'd ever had. Shaking, she swallowed and licked at her lips, still breathing hard as she tried to still her racing heart. In the future, she would much rather he beat her.

ILAR'S BODY WAS STIFF FROM DENIAL. HE RESENTED every aching, torturous second of it. If he thought it would help, he would have tried to ease himself from the pain. But he knew there was no use. He could self-pleasure himself a million times and with one thought of Lady Rhiannon, he would rise anew. He didn't like his will being taken away from him like this. He didn't like attacking women, especially without thought. He wasn't a monster. But he had acted like one.

Closing his eyes, he still felt her, smelled her, heard her. He tasted her blood on his lips, flavored with a tingle of hesitant longing. She wasn't immune to him. She might be terrified, but she wasn't immune. It didn't please him to know that if he wanted, he could seduce her to his bed. It made the temptation to do so that much worse.

"How is your prisoner?" Larus frowned, seeing his Commander's blood tinged eyes. By the howling in his head, the king surely knew nothing had happened—well, at least nothing had finished—between the human prisoner and her lycan keeper.

"We should lock the men in the prisons," Ilar stated gruffly. It was a bold suggestion. His eyes swam with gold and he didn't bother to control it. He didn't have the energy left in him.

Larus lifted a brow. He uncrossed his legs and moved to stand. The main hall was quiet. He had banished all men from that half of the castle to separate them from the siren. It hadn't helped. Their cries grew with each passing hour. "Do you think you overreact?"

"She's too potent. The cries get worse," Ilar said, tortured. He pressed his hands into his temples, trying to drown out the sounds. The only time he had any peace from the screaming was when he touched Rhiannon, and that only brought a worse torture. "You have not smelled her so you cannot understand. The curse grows, strengthens. We need to imprison the guards who have been affected by her if only to protect them from themselves. Their minds grow obsessed with her at each passing moment."

"And you?" Larus asked, eyeing Ilar's rigid body and pumping fists, as they clenched and unclenched in growing agitation. The Commander jerked as he moved. He fought hard for his control. "Do you need to be imprisoned?"

Ilar swallowed. His eyes rolled in his head as he thought about her. "I will be fine. I need a moment to recuperate. She took me off guard. I will not let it happen again. Besides, someone has to keep watch over her."

"You do not look well," Larus put forth. Indeed, his friend was looking a little gray. "Are you sure I shouldn't send another to tend her?"

Ilar scowled, not liking the idea of another being in her presence, another tempted to kiss her, another tempted to touch her soft body. Growling a bit too harshly, he stated, "No. I will tend to her. She's my responsibility."

Larus was taken aback by the swift possessiveness that came with the statement. Slowly, he nodded his head. "All right, it will be as you wish. But, if I think she's affecting your judgment, I'll lock you away with the others."

Ilar nodded, not answering. He couldn't. His mind was beginning to drift to the key he kept in his tunic. It'd be so easy to go back up there and claim her. The temptation was great. Surely it would end this madness if he just...

It was unthinkable.

"I have sent the unmated women away to Fenris. They aggravated the men with their bloodlust. I sent word to Malak that he was to receive them and watch them." Larus sighed. Ilar didn't seem to be listening. His head was turned to the ceiling in the direction of the mortal.

To the king's surprise, Ilar answered, "Very wise. Malak will undoubtedly be happy to have his court overrun with women. For a man who does not wish for a lifemate, he sure takes pleasure in having women around him."

"We could send him this woman," Larus mused, teasing. He was rewarded with a dark, overprotective snarl. The king's brows furrowed. He'd seen the affected men. They didn't have that same gleam to their eyes. With the others, it was pure, hot, animalistic lust that boiled within them. With Ilar, it appeared to be something more. Larus frowned. Maybe being in proximity to the human was having a harder effect on the Commander.

"I wouldn't risk taking her back out in the open," Ilar answered instead, never realizing Larus was joking. He again stared at the ceiling. Hearing a new wave of anguish invading his pounding head, he added, "You had better put them into separate cells, lest they take it to mind to battle."

Larus nodded in silent agreement.

Sighing heavily as a wave of yearning washed over him anew, Ilar grumbled to the king, "I am going to the practice field. I need to burn off this energy."

Larus watched his friend storm away, twitching angrily as he moved. The king tried to use the mind link to call to the mated guards to start rounding up the affected ones. The mind link was full of lustful howls and he cursed. Striding across the main hall of the castle, Larus went to find them for himself.

Rhiannon eyed the empty tray with satisfaction. She had finished off every last bite of food and her stomach thanked her repeatedly with contented purrs and gurgles of pleasure. She'd been famished, more so than she'd realized. Taking up a wooden goblet, she finished the last of the sweet berry wine as well.

Her stomach filled, she yawned, stretching her hands over her head. From the looks of the dark purple sky outside, it had to be getting later in the day. She studied the large bed, debating only a little, before crawling onto its thick inviting folds. The fresh bedding was warm from the fireplace and she nestled contentedly beneath the coverlet and linens, burrowing into the soft mattress. Within moments, she was fast asleep.

Cupid's wrinkled troll face lit with pleasure to see the havoc he wrought on all of Lycaon. Ah, revenge had never been sweeter. His arms pumped into the air. He was eager for the day he could reveal to Lord Ilar that it was he who entranced the entire Lycan Guard, bringing them to their knees with burning lust.

Seeing the howling men being dragged off to the prisons, he did a little jig of glee, dancing unnoticed over the tower wall. The lycan brawled amongst themselves and even Ilar had to break up his fair share of the fights.

Lord Ilar wasn't immune to the human. He detected the Commander's dark look from across the bailey yard. The potion worked so much better than planned. Rubbing his hands together, Cupid chuckled. It wouldn't be long until Ilar mated himself to the disgusting mortal. Then the spell would be broken and Ilar would see what he had done.

Cupid laughed louder, a delighted sound. His stubby

legs pumped faster beneath his dirt covered breeches. All of a sudden, he stubbed his toe on a jutted rock and tripped off the wall. Tumbling head over feet, the troll landed hard on his stomach and banged his overlarge nose.

THE AFFECTED LYCANS WERE PUT INTO THE PRISONS. Ilar didn't have a choice. He'd broken up their fights all evening. Some had even been so bold as to challenge him for his position. It wasn't a challenge he could refuse, but he could put it off until a later date. Hopefully, the foolish men would retract their words and Ilar wouldn't be forced to rip their throats from their necks.

Those who hadn't smelled the human were unaltered, but the disturbance in the mind link made the remaining men boorish and short of temper. They didn't relish imprisoning their comrades to accommodate a mere human. There were several who even went so far as to suggest they kill the mortal intruder and be done with it. Ilar only stayed their intent by saying that the curse was so strong the others might want her even in death.

The idea was so distasteful that the call for an execution was immediately withdrawn.

As he made his way resignedly to his bedchamber, Ilar knew he was a glutton for punishment. He should spend the night alone in one of the guest rooms, but he didn't want to chance there being an attack on the mortal while he slept. The only way to ensure Rhiannon's safety throughout the night was to be by her side. It was going to be pure hell.

To his surprise, she was already asleep on his bed when he came into the room. Her lips were parted in rest. He instantly remembered their soft texture against his mouth. She looked like an angel, her long golden curls twisting around her oval face, spilling softly over her shoulders and breasts. She still wore the green tunic gown, and it hugged to her curves, tangling with the bedcovers she'd thrown from her body. Her bare feet hung off the side of the bed.

All of a sudden, he frowned. Stalking noiselessly around the bed, he looked at her feet. The soles were bruised and several angry scratches puckered along the bottoms. How had he not noticed it before? Seeing an angry gash on her arch, curling around the side, he knew she must have gotten the injury as he dragged her to Lycaon from the stream. She hadn't complained once. Eyeing her with grudging respect, he realized she was much tougher than he had been willing to give her credit for.

Going to his trunk, he searched the contents for a salve. He rarely used the healing cream and had a hard time finding it. Finally, discovering a *fisyk* at the bottom corner, he pulled it out. Grabbing a chair, he moved it to the side of the bed and sat by her feet.

With a light finger, he stroked the cream over her wounds. Her foot twitched slightly at the touch, but she didn't awaken. Ilar concentrated on his task, being extra sensitive of the deeper gashes. When hc finished his painstaking care, he glanced at her. Her blue eyes were open, staring at him in sleepy puzzlement.

He frowned at being caught. Lifting the small jar, he stated, "It will help."

Rhiannon glanced at her feet and slowly drew them back onto the bed, away from him. She hadn't forgotten their last meeting. The proof of it was still marred on her bottom lip. Swallowing, as if frightened more by his tenderness than his gruff ways, she said weakly, "Thank you."

Ilar didn't like her softening tone and quickly stood. He threw the jar unceremoniously into the trunk. "Do not read too much into it. You are my prisoner and I'm duty bound to make sure you stay relatively healthy."

"Prisoner," she repeated, her mind seeming to linger

on that one word. The pleasure faded from her features to be replaced by ire. She rolled her eyes heavenward at him. Turning on the bed, so her back faced him, she stated, "Well, if you are done, get out of my prison. I want to sleep."

"This is my chamber," he said.

It took a moment for his words to enter her troubled mind. When they did, she shot up on the bed. Looking him over, she clutched the covers to her chest as if he meant to attack that very instant.

"You cannot sleep here," she denied. Then, lacking any better defense, she added, "It is not... proper."

"Again, mortal," he mused, delighting in the way her face darkened in anger at the word *mortal*. "You have no say here. And propriety does not concern masters and their prisoners. I'm afraid you have no choice in the matter."

"W-well," she stammered weakly.

To her horror, he unclasped the brooch on his shoulder and swung the draping tunic off his body. The material slid to the floor, leaving him naked. Her eyes instantly took in his firm backside.

Ilar stretched his arms over his head. He grinned, instinctively knowing she would be watching as he gave her a little show. His tight, bronzed body flexed wickedly as his weight shifted, dimpling the cheek in the most roguish of ways. The muscles drew up along his spine as he moved.

A creeping blush made Rhiannon turn away to hide beneath a veil of blonde curls. Belatedly, she finished, proving to Ilar that he'd been right—she had been watching. "Yo-you cannot mean to sleep in the bed with me."

"This is my bed," he stated. He turned to her, comfortable in his nakedness. He flung the covers back and made a move to crawl slowly in. Again, he kept his movements purposeful, stalking, flexing ever so slightly in all the right ways to draw her eyes where he wanted them. Her round gaze dutifully traveled where he wished it to, making their heated way over his form.

Rhiannon gasped in noisy protest when he drew nearer, a smile on his parted lips. A strange tingling began on her skin. She tried to edge off the side, away from him.

Ilar watched her tremble in the most modest way he had ever seen. He darted his hand out, keeping her from escaping the bed. He pulled her by her hips into his naked embrace.

"Where are you going?" he asked, lowering his tone into a playful murmur. She instantly stiffened.

"I'll sleep on the floor," she announced, but her words lacked conviction. "If you are not gentleman enough to... then... I..."

His eyes moved slowly over her and she knew he didn't hear her words. The firm press of his muscles fitted along her side. The tunic gown offered little protection from his heat as he inched her closer. He caressed his hands against her stomach in absent circles, moving intimately over her hip.

Ilar let her feel his body against hers. Her protests faded until she merely stared at him. Her mouth worked as if it still spoke, but nothing came from her throat but a soft pant.

Ah, he thought, *much better.*

Ilar continued to touch her, discovering her form with confident, expert hands. He moved his fingers boldly over her neck, her breasts, her hips and thighs. He cupped her cheek, traced the swoop of her throat, down the front of her chest. He wanted to kiss her, but held back, liking the way her eyes drifted closed in pleasure. A dreamy sigh whispered past her lips. He grabbed a fistful of her skirt, working the material up. When her thighs were exposed, he fitted his heavy erection along her leg, watching her closely for a reaction.

Rhiannon's eyes widened, and she did her best not to scream for help. He rocked his hips into her. She watched him, studied him, tried to read his mind to discover his thoughts. All she could do was feel him.

Ilar growled, dipping his head close to her, as he let

himself have the pleasure of sniffing her intoxicating smell. His engorged shaft rubbed lightly into her leg, desiring nothing more than to stroke into her slick depths. Instinctively, he knew she'd be ready for him.

Leaning close to her ear, he let his breath send waves of pleasure over her skin. His hand drifted to a breast, rubbing it lightly through the cloth. His voice rumbled in a way that had melted many females before her. "I like touching you, Rhian, and I know you like it when I touch you."

Rhiannon stopped breathing and a little shiver worked over her. Ilar licked ever so lightly at her earlobe. A weak sound escaped her. It felt too good to push him away, so she merely lay still, letting him have his way. His mouth lifted to hers. He edged his tongue, seductively firm and rough, into the part of her lips, his eyes looking directly into hers.

Rhiannon whimpered. It felt like a stampede of wild horses ran over her chest, thundering and pounding where her heart should have been.

Against her lips, he said, "*Mm*, I like tasting you. I want to taste all of you."

Rhiannon's heart again stopped beating. Forget the horses. She was positive he had killed her with that last statement. He was the devil, and she was dead, only this didn't feel like eternal damnation.

"Tell me you want to stay in my bed," he urged, licking and kissing at her mouth as he spoke. "Say the words. Tell me you want me to taste you, touch you, feel you, claim you. Tell me to come inside you, Rhian."

Rhiannon wanted nothing more than to repeat his words back to him. Finding her last shred of dignity, she said, "No. I am a prisoner."

Ilar forced a smile, though his body stung with tight rejection. Instantly, he released her breast, leaving her with an unbearable ache. Rolling away from her, he declared, as if it didn't distress him to leave her, "So be it, Rhiannon. It will be as you wish."

Rhiannon closed her eyes tight as he spoke. She almost recanted, but then he grabbed the pillow from beneath her head and jerked it out from under her. She blinked in surprise.

Ilar threw the pillow on the floor before the fire. Then, taking the coverlet, he did the same. Looking at her expectantly, he motioned to the floor.

Rhiannon balked as she got his meaning. He was kicking her off the bed onto the floor. Angrily, she shot her darkest look at him and threw the remaining covers from her legs. Ilar smiled angelically in return and made a great show of spreading his limbs over the full length of the comfortable mattress. Not bothering to hide his still potent erection as it tangled in the covers, he heaved a pleasured sigh for her benefit.

Rhiannon stormed from the bed, stopping furiously before the fire. Grabbing the coverlet, she wrapped it around her arms and made herself a place on the hard stone. Already her aching body begged her to return to the bed, but to do so would be to allow Ilar to touch her, to take her. That was something she couldn't permit.

"Good eve, Lady Rhian," Ilar said softly, leaning up on his elbows to look at her.

Her mouth pressed tightly in anger, refusing to answer. She stared at the ceiling rafters.

Feigning a contented sigh, he lay down and murmured, "You know where I am if you change your mind."

Ilar swore he heard her mumble something about skinning him for a fur rug to decorate his chamber. He almost lost himself to laughter.

"*Arrrgh. I'll break through your door,* Commander, if you don't give me the woman. I want her. I want to claim her for myself!"

Ilar's eyes opened, hearing the growl resounding from outside the bedchamber door. His eyes narrowed, sensing his fellow lycan's discontent. The growl sounded again, followed by a desperate pounding. Someone tried frantically to get inside his locked bedchamber.

"Give her to me." the voice roared. "I want her."

Rhiannon awoke from her place on the floor and shot up in fright, just in time to see Ilar leaping naked out of the bed. She gasped at the sight of his powerful form and would have blushed if not for the continued yelling of whoever fought to get inside the chamber. She blinked, terrified, unable to understand what the man said. Soon the shouts turned to bestial growls.

Ilar felt the man shifting as he struggled to get past the thick oak door to Rhiannon. He growled menacingly in return, using the mind link to send the soldier warnings. It didn't work. The young lycan was beyond hearing him. He was possessed by the smell of the human. To Ilar's distress, he realized the lycan not only lusted to mate with her, but he lusted for her blood. If the young one got to Rhiannon, he would slaughter her as he mated with her.

Realizing Ilar planned on unlocking the door to the intruder, Rhiannon jumped to her feet, "Ilar, no."

Too late.

He threw open the door, ready for the attack. The young soldier lunged over his shoulder, his wolf jaw snapping viciously as he tried to leap onto Rhiannon. She screamed and ran across the room in complete terror. The wolf growled, barking in displeasure.

Ilar lifted his arm at the last minute to stop the young lycan's progress. Striking him in the neck, he flung him back out into the hall. Calling over his shoulder, as he went to grab the impertinent guard up, he ordered, "Rhian, lock the door behind me and open it for no one else."

Rhiannon didn't have to be told twice. Scurrying to

the door, she slammed it shut, seeing only a glimpse of Ilar's naked form as he dragged the unconscious beast behind him by the tail.

Shivering, she sat alongside the door, leaning her ear against the wood to listen for sounds. Her body was stiff from the night spent on the hard stone, but she didn't feel it. The image of Ilar's lunging form stayed with her. He had protected her.

ILAR LIFTED THE WARRIOR ONTO HIS SHOULDER, adjusting the weight in irritation, as he stormed down his tower steps to the main hall. A group of lycans blinked to see their naked Commander carrying the unconscious guard, before turning guiltily away. They were the only ones in the main hall and Ilar strode straight for them.

"What are you doing in here?" Ilar demanded. "Let me see your eyes. Has she affected you?"

They frowned, confused. Ilar looked them over, sniffing them. They appeared unaltered.

"Why was this man at my door?" Ilar demanded, bouncing the load on his shoulder with ease. The unconscious lycan's weight was nothing to the Commander's strength.

"We were having a bit of fun," one of the men

answered, his gray eyes cast down sheepishly. "He was bragging how he wasn't afraid of the—"

"So you challenged him to my door?" Ilar roared, incensed. "Do you think this is a game? He nearly got himself killed, and he wanted to kill the woman."

The soldiers looked at their leader in disbelief, thinking him to be overly possessive of the female.

"It's just a human," a blond man tried to defend.

"Just a human?" Ilar shot, gently laying the wolf down at their feet. "You have no idea what this human is capable of. She'll take your mind from you. Make you insane. She's cursed and she will curse any who come near her. This is not a game."

"But, you—" one of the men began, skeptical.

"You think me unharmed?" Ilar snarled. His eyes turned wildly at them and he balled his hands into fists. Instantly, they understood their mistake. Ilar wasn't so unaffected as they had believed. "There is a prison full of your brethren that are as unharmed as I am."

"Yes, Commander," they all mumbled, nodding at the reprimand. They looked despairingly at the fallen man.

Ilar placed his hands on his naked hips. His eyes glared with molten gold as he stared them down. He knew they'd been teasing each other, daring the youngest to prove himself. "Get him to the dungeons with the others and lock him away where he can do no harm. And so help me, the next one of you that comes to my door without being summoned will not be leaving it. Is that understood?"

The men nodded, leaning over to pick up the unconscious wolf. Ilar growled at them, a truly bestial sound.

"And stay out of this hall," Ilar yelled to their departing backs. Spinning on his heels, he stopped, seeing Larus watching from the side passage. Larus said nothing, turning away from him.

Ilar took the tower steps two at a time. When he reached the door, he forced himself to slow. Taking a deep breath, he tried the latch. Rhiannon had obeyed him. The door was locked from within.

Now that he was alone, he took another deep breath. He'd been worried when he first heard the young guard's attack. He didn't want to tell Larus, but there was bloodlust in the warrior's eyes—the ancient curse of the lycan, one that wasn't stirred too often. Ilar frowned. He'd felt it too, only he didn't want to admit it. Even in his dreams he'd tasted the drop of blood he'd pierced from her mouth.

Whatever the curse, it was getting stronger and harder to resist.

Quietly, he knocked on the door, "Rhiannon, open the door."

He heard a small shuffle and then silence.

"Rhian?" he called, trying to keep the raggedness out of his words, though he wanted nothing more than to plow through the wood and grab her to him, making sure she was safe. "It is I, Ilar. You are safe. He will not harm you."

"Ilar?" she called shakily. Suddenly, the door was unlatched, and she moved to peek through the crack. Seeing that it was truly him, she sighed in heavy relief.

Ilar pushed his way in, turning to lock the door behind him. She blushed when she saw he was still without clothes.

"Is he...?" she began. Biting at her lips, she moaned faintly. "Is he dead?"

"No," Ilar stated, studying her. If he wasn't mistaken, she almost seemed relieved to hear it. "But he won't be coming back here."

Rhiannon nodded. "Is it because he hates humans that he wants me dead?"

Ilar frowned. He didn't want to tell her the truth, or else she might find a way to turn her charm against them to escape. If she even tried to seduce them, she'd conquer them all. Her timid fear was the only defense they had against her.

Rhiannon took his silence to mean that she was right in assuming so. There had been so much passion in the wolf. She had no idea they hated her so much.

"Ilar…" Tears entered her eyes. "I want to help you. I want to find who brought me here. I'll tell you everything. Only, in return, I'll have your promise that I'll be brought home unharmed when this is over."

Ilar stood silent, studying her. Such a promise wasn't his to give. "I promise to protect you."

Rhiannon almost swooned with relief to hear it. She believed him. "Why do you hate humans so much?"

"It is an old feud," he murmured, not wanting to get into it. "Your kind tried to destroy mine. There was a battle and afterward, our worlds separated."

"I haven't heard of such a battle," Rhiannon said in disbelief. She sat on the bed.

"It was nigh three hundred years ago," Ilar answered. "In the human world, things have a way of becoming myths over such a time."

"How do you know it's true? Perhaps it has become a myth in your world, as well," she reasoned.

Ilar gave a short, humorless laugh. "I was there."

Rhiannon's eyes widened as she got his meaning. She licked her lips, somewhat glancing down his body before catching herself. All she managed was, "Oh."

Ilar noticed that she tried hard not to look at him. A slow smile came to his lips.

"Does my nakedness bother you?" he asked, his tone lowering into a seductive murmur. She was so easy to tease and he found himself enjoying making her blush. Lycan women were sexually aggressive like the men. To see this timid human hiding from her desire amazed and fascinated him.

Rhiannon shivered. Her mouth worked to answer. "I wasn't going to say... anything, but you should cover that... yourself."

Her cheeks turned a bright, fiery red. Ilar's body continued to stir now that the conflict was over. He took a step closer to her. She stiffened. He grinned.

"It isn't..." Rhiannon moaned, making a weak sound in the back of her throat. She tried to stand as he neared. But as he stepped in her way, she was forced to sit back down. Completely aware that his hips were dangerously close to her face, she turned from him and leaned away. In a whisper, she finished ineffectually, "proper."

Ilar grinned. He knew she was trying hard to ignore his erection. He wasn't as embarrassed about his body as she clearly was. His desire was a most natural occurrence —well, aside from the curse on her, it was natural. He couldn't help it or himself, as he knew he had to provoke her. His accent grew thick with need, as he inquired, "Do you want to touch me? Do you want to feel me?"

Rhiannon gasped, turning her round eyes to his

mirthful ones. Her lips pulled stiffly, as she obviously lied, "N-no."

Ilar took another step forward. Whispering down to her, he let his finger hover near her face without feeling her. "No one will know of it. Go ahead. Touch my body."

Oh, but it was a tempting offer. Rhiannon swallowed nervously. It was an offer she wouldn't dare to take. She glanced at him again, seeing his wide smile. He was teasing her.

"Touch me," he urged. His built arms pulled across his chest, challenging her, daring her to turn weakly away.

"Fine," she huffed. With a slap, she hit his naked stomach hard and shoved him back. Hissing under her breath, she said, "There, now go get dressed."

"Do you not wish to look at me?" he murmured, stepping once more before her, unharmed by her blow. He let his arms fall to the side, offering himself up for inspection. "Look your fill, Rhian. I don't mind. I want you to look at me. I want to see what my body does to you."

"I-I..." Rhiannon's throat went dry and she couldn't stop herself from accepting his invitation. Her gaze met his dark, piercing eyes. A slow wolfish smile curved his lips, drawing her eyes to his delightfully wicked mouth. His long hair fell over his back and chest in long waves. He held still and her eyes drifted hesitantly lower. His formidable chest strained with muscles beneath the sun-bronzed flesh. She remembered too easily the feel of its hardness pressed to her skin.

She swallowed, closing her eyes briefly before moving them down. Ilar thought he would explode at the rate her gaze traveled, taking in every nuance of him.

Rhiannon was tense, waiting for a laugh or a sneer that never came. The rippling movement of his stomach caught her attention, moving with each deep breath he drew. A trail of dark hair led her down from his navel to his most private of areas. His arousal was full, straining with little veins bulging down the smooth sides, embedded in soft hair. Two heavy globes hung under-neath. They too appeared to strain. Her mouth opened, and she was unable to draw her eyes away.

"May I look at you?" he asked after a long moment, surprised and pleased that she hadn't backed away from his challenge so far.

Rhiannon's eyes finally managed to seek something other than his thick arousal as they moved to his hand-some face. His dark eyes shifted with gold flecks, glowing with what could have been humor or something much, much darker in purpose. Thinking he'd gone mad, she said, "You are looking at me."

"May I look at all of you?" he persisted, coming closer. His eyes were a little dazed and his features pulled strangely. Before she knew what was happening, he had his lips gently to hers and was pushing her back on the bed with brushing kisses to her lips and jaw. Groaning against her, he inquired, "May I taste you, Rhian? May I taste all of you?"

Rhiannon jolted in surprise, whimpering lightly. Ilar dipped his tongue to hers, massaging her mouth at great length without pressing his lips deeply to hers. She shivered, gasped, moaned. Only his mouth felt her. He tried to burn his passion into her body through her swollen lips.

Rhiannon fell back on the bed and away from his kiss, too weak to remain up. His eyes raged as they pierced down into her. He was so handsome, so breathtaking. Her heart sped in wicked excitement. Even though she knew it was wrong, she didn't want him to stop.

Slowly, his head tilted, and he looked down over her side. He fitted his hands lightly to her hip, trailing over her leg. He inched her skirt up, baring her calves. Her hair spilled forth over her shoulders, haloing around her head. Her body looked so soft, so warm and inviting.

"May I feel you, Rhian?" he asked, his eyes smoldering into her with their seriousness. He moved his fingers to start a haphazard journey up her inner leg, reaching the bend of her knee before falling flat to her skin. His caresses became more profound as he massaged his way to the awaiting apex of her thighs. "Tell me you want me, Rhian. Tell me you want me to come to you."

"Ilar," she gasped. "Oh, you mustn't—*ah.*"

He inched his fingers higher, watching, smelling her response to him. Her body arched slightly as he intimately stroked into her. Her fists tightened along her sides as if she would keep them from reaching for him.

"Shh," he said quietly, drawing closer. He worked his hand against her hip, teasing her nether hair as he moved. He watched her, his eyes hot. He took deep breaths as he fought for control. "I want to feel you, Rhian. I want to touch you."

As he said the words, his finger slipped to her sex. To his masculine pleasure, she was hot and wet without having to be coaxed. Slowly, he traced the delicate lips, parting her folds so he could feel the hidden silk of her body.

Rhiannon delicately jerked at the feel of his strong hand. She beckoned him down to her, reaching her hands to him, wanting to explore him. She was mindless to anything but the hand that moved against her, stirring a terrible ache that was so pleasurable in its torment.

"Ilar," she moaned. She found his neck and lodged her fingers into his hair, pulling him closer, seeking his heat. Offering her breasts, she arched her back only to rub her hips up into him. She pulled him to her. His lips found her throat, kissing beneath her ear and then biting the lobe. He inched his finger to delve deep inside her.

Ilar groaned. Her thighs stiffened against his hand, trying to stop him. She was no match for his strength. Slowly, he pushed forward, all the time licking and kissing at her throat and jaw, nearly consuming her with his passion for her. He let her hear his ragged breath as it fell hot against her flesh. He eased his finger to stroke her, liking the way her muscles gripped him tightly. She clutched at his shoulders, pulling and pushing in confusion.

"Ah," he sighed, liking the feel of her very much. "Relax yourself to me, Rhian. I want to feel deeper. Let my finger glide in the cream your body has made for me."

Rhiannon tried to obey. It was a glorious agony his finger wrought. Her breath caught as he coaxed himself within her, his finger beginning to move, withdrawing.

"Oh, Ilar, please," she begged, not knowing what she wanted. She drew over his shoulders and arms, urging him to her, gripping his flesh.

Ilar grunted. His body became tight. When he again delved inside, he used two fingers opening her even more to him. "Ah, you're so tight. I want to stretch you."

"Ilar," she trembled against the fullness, becoming aware. He stroked her, pulling and pushing with agonizing slowness. The fingers inside her curled and moved. His thumb was circling her top arch, flicking at the sensitive nub. "We... you can't do this. You have to stop."

She was right, of course.

"Ugh," he grumbled, pulling back. Her cream was on his fingers, sliding effortlessly on his flesh. He took his mouth from her neck. Harsh from denial, he looked down into her impassioned features and agreed, "Fine."

Rhiannon jolted in surprise. He wasn't actually supposed to stop. *Now* he decided to listen to her?

Ilar pulled back from her. The look on her face was almost worth the agonizing pain in his gut. Almost. But it wasn't like he could finish this little game like he wanted to.

"What are you doing?" she asked, breathless. She watched his naked body cross over to his trunk. With a toss of his arms, he was dressed in dark blue and pinning a circular brooch at his shoulder. Rhiannon quickly covered her legs, wondering at the spasm of anger in her womb.

When he turned to her, he said, "I go to check on the fallen soldier."

In truth, he was going to get away from her. He was a man of infinite control, but even his willpower wore thin when he was around her. One more torturous second within her sweet, tight passage and he would have taken her—willing or no.

Cupid watched Ilar coming down from the tower. The troll glared at the lycan as he rubbed the tip of his bruised nose. He crouched down and hid behind the leg of a table as he waited for the Commander to pass.

All the affected men had been locked away so there was no fun to be had outside, no fighting or combat. Ilar proved himself immune to the woman, or else he'd have mated to her already. The potion's effect should not have taken so long. The only way Ilar could have resisted was if he and the ugly human were soul mates, but even then he should have been mindless with passion. Cupid laughed. Now, that would be funny. Not that he wished to have a hand in finding Ilar a soul mate.

Waddling across the empty hall, he looked up at the tower stairs. Pulling on the back of his breeches, he vigorously scratched his inflamed backside. When the itch wouldn't be tamed, he reached beneath the dirty material with his tiny, gnarled hand and began dancing in circles to get the job done. His feet kicked as high as they could go as he hopped about the clean stone floor.

When he'd finished, Cupid frowned, rubbing his

beady eye. He had no desire to see the ugly mortal again, but it looked as if he had no choice. Lord Ilar kept her locked away tighter than the leprechauns locked up their precious gold—and Cupid should know, he'd tried to steal some once.

13

Rhiannon paced the floor of Ilar's bedchamber, trying to get control of her emotions. Her cheeks flamed as she remembered what his body felt like against hers. She could still taste his kiss on her lips and, though she told herself she hated every minute of it, she wanted to try more. Oh, and how she wished his hand hadn't stopped.

Halting in her frantic movements, she stared defiantly at the firelight. Did she actually think that? Did she wish to have the *nieten* touch her? To her dismay, she knew the answer was yes, she did. It was so wrong, but she liked his frightening power. She appreciated that he wasn't like the men of her world. There was a raw power to him as if passion boiled beneath a refined surface. Though refined wasn't precisely the right word either. She saw the gentleman in him but wondered how much of it was real and how much an illusion to hide the creature he carried within. Rhiannon liked the bold way he stared at her with liquid dark eyes that swam with golden swirls. Her father would be horrified if he ever discovered what she'd allowed to happen. He'd turn her from the castle, from her family.

"Ah, so sad, little sparrow caught in her cage, cannot fly away. Poor, poor sparrow."

Rhiannon froze, not making any sudden movements. She knew that taunting, shrill voice. It pricked at her memory.

"Trapped in her cage, wings broken by a beast."

"Who are you?" Rhiannon asked cautiously. She kept her eye steadily on the flames, trying to reach out with her senses for movement or sound. There was only the continued grating of the voice.

"A friend," the irritating resonance answered, nearing a cackle at the words. "A friend come to take you from your cage, broken sparrow."

"Show yourself if you are truly my friend," Rhiannon demanded. Her heart pounded. She tried not to think of Ilar or the pain she felt at leaving him.

"Turn around and you will see," the callous voice said, "and I will take you home."

Rhiannon slowly obeyed, her eyes gliding over the

chamber to the bed. She gasped, pulling back in horror. Lounging on the bed with his grubby feet kicked out, rested a squat, wrinkly creature unlike any she'd ever seen. Her nose curled as she caught a horrific scent wafting from him.

"What are you?" she asked, her brow furrowed in disgust.

"I've come to free you from your prison, sparrow," the repulsive creature said.

To her horror, he picked at his nose, only to lick his finger. Rhiannon gagged, flinching as bile rose in her throat.

"Come with me, little sparrow, and I'll take you from here." The man stood on the bed. With great effort, he walked over the soft mattress, wobbling on his short legs. His fat lips stretched wide, nearly encompassing his whole face. He jumped from the bed with little grace and waddled to the door. Waving his hand, he beckoned, "Come, before the beast gets back."

"I cannot go out there," Rhiannon denied. "They want to kill me."

"Kill you?" Cupid asked in surprise, his eyes narrowing in wonder. He studied the woman before him, trying not to flinch at her clean smell and her ugly face. "Who would want to kill you?"

"The lycans," she explained. "They hate humans. I cannot go out there."

"The lycans?" Cupid exclaimed, feigning surprise at the very thought. "The lycans love humans, worship them like gods."

"But...?" Rhiannon's brows furrowed in confusion. Her body still reeled from Ilar's touch. Even now, she could feel his fingers on her, in her, mystifying her.

"Ah," Cupid said, nodding his head sadly. He hit his neck as a flea bit him. "The lycan that pretended to attack you, you mean. He drinks now with Lord Ilar. A merry game they think to play with you. Evil Lord Ilar. He thinks to keep a goddess captured in his chambers. He thinks you will bring him luck, human sparrow."

"What do you mean evil?" she asked, seeing the creature's forlorn face. Ilar did have the look of a devil to him, but she never really thought of him as evil. She might have called him that, but she'd been sick with cold and never truly believed it.

"He found you and means to make you his..." Cupid affected a frown.

"He means to make me his... take me to his bed?" Rhiannon finished, her face becoming hard.

"Aye, that," Cupid said with a solemn nod of his head. "That he does so he too will be worshiped by the lycans." Cupid affected a pout. "He uses you, human.

He told the wolf to attack you to make you stay inside, frightened. He means to keep you prisoner to his bed. He's playing with you. It's what the lycans sometimes do. Come on. I got you into this. I'll get you out."

"Wait a minute," Rhiannon said. "How can I trust you? You're the one who scared me in my chamber. You hit me in the head and brought me here."

"No, no, my lady," Cupid said. "A spell went wrong, and you were brought to this world. I've come to take you back to yours. A mistake only, please lady sparrow, come. Let us be gone. Make haste before the devil comes back. His patience grows thin, ever so thin. Lord Ilar won't be put off much longer."

Ilar frowned, spinning around on his heels in distraction to see who dared disrupt his rampage. Spying a dark face and wavy raven black hair nearly as long as his own, he frowned good-naturedly. "Malak, what brings you to this accursed place? Why are you not at Fenris?"

"You send all your angry women to my door and expect me to stay away?" Malak grinned. His chest was bare as he never fastened his tunic over his shoulder, preferring to let it lay about his trim waist. Ilar was sure he did it to attract the women. It appeared to work, for he had an overabundance of females vying for his companionship.

"I expected you to stay at Fenris and enjoy the gift," Ilar said, grumpily.

"Enjoy your present, I did." Malak looked over his old friend's face with amusement. Oh, he'd enjoyed the present aplenty. In fact, he still had the bite marks on his hip to prove it. However, he'd heard the rumors that Ilar had locked a human woman in his chambers, and the guards had been locked into prison. Malak had to see for himself. "By the way, the men wished me to thank you. The women's blood is stirred to boiling and they mate with them like mad and with little provoking or care. Never has my keep been so thoroughly sated. Alas, nothing is getting done for they are all abed..." Malak waved his hand absently. He shrugged as if to say, *but what can we do?*

Ilar grunted. At least someone was mating. The practice field was near empty as they approached it.

"Pleasurable as it was to be given the most unusual forms of gratification at every turn, I couldn't bring myself to stay away from such an intriguing occurrence. Will you let me see her?" Malak asked, getting straight to the point. A roguish smile lit on his face. "If she's as beautiful as they say, I will gladly take her as my lover. If you are not man enough to end this castle's torment, I will do it."

"Since when does the woman have to be pretty for you to mate with her?" Ilar grumbled, knowing Malak teased him. Malak hardly took anything seriously. "I seem to recall you mated with a dwarf once."

"Ah, she was a small elf, not a dwarf," Malak broke in, forcing a scowl.

Ilar chuckled, despite his black mood. He glanced around the clean bailey yard. Soldiers walked over the battlements, their eyes stretching out over the distance. A cool breeze whipped over the bailey, refreshing in the hotter sunlight.

"Believe me," Ilar said roughly, shaking his head. "Even you will want none of this wench. She's an enchanted mortal."

15

Rhiannon followed the troll out of the bedchamber and down the tower steps. Her limbs shook with fear at what she might find. She hoped the strange little being was right, that the lycans didn't wish to harm her. But, really, what other choice did she have than to follow him? Ilar didn't seem to know how to get her home and this was the creature that had brought her from her realm. Though he was disgusting, his words sounded sincere.

Besides, hadn't Ilar already told her he planned on publicly making her his whore? She stiffened in anger to discover that he was staying true to his word. He was using her for his own gain. It hurt that his touch was nothing more than a play for power when she felt him branded on every corner of her soul.

The smelly troll glanced over his shoulder to watch her as he led her through the barren hall. She tried to smile, but he turned back too quickly. Rhiannon looked around, eyeing the clean keep. Banners hung down over the walls and, except for a few changes, it looked very much like the castles back home.

Well, except for him, she thought, eyeing the troll.

Waving his hand, the creature tried to speed their progression as he hopped and ran at the same time to the bailey yard. Frightened that Ilar might come along and discover her, she crept closer to the troll. Smelling his disgusting scent, she thought better of it and backed away once more.

Rhiannon glanced over the empty area she hardly remembered passing through on her way inside the castle. It was eerie in its quiet as if abandoned. Leading her to the battlements, the troll looked up and grinned in mischief.

She frowned upon seeing the troll stopped. She followed his gaze up to the battlements.

"Why do you stop?" she asked, frantic. She tried to find what he looked for.

Cupid shivered as he impatiently waved a hand to keep her quiet. He was having a hard time stomaching her clean smell and her fresh, rosy looks. They made him nauseous. It was apparent Agrona had gotten the beauty in that family. Edging along the wall, he listened, barely making a sound.

Rhiannon detected swift movement along the battlements, blurring against the purplish skyline. A man leapt from the high wall, landing gracefully before her on both feet. The fall should have hurt him, but he crouched only slightly before standing tall. His eyes blazed with golden heat as he looked her over, his gaze all too possessive for a stranger. Rhiannon turned, intent on running.

"Hold." the troll ordered. He clapped his hands lightly. Rhiannon obeyed, stiffening to her place on the ground. The man's eyes roamed over her, his nose lifting to the air to sniff at her. She glanced at the troll. He grinned, nearly teeming with pleasure to see the lycan. He leaned over and grabbed a stick as he sidled next to her. Placing the stick in her hand, he said, "Throw this and order him to fetch it for you."

Rhiannon slowly drew the stick up, readying a throw. Before she could even let go, two more lycan men hopped down from the wall, turning to face her. Their eyes were the same, possessive and flaming, glittering with the look of molten gold. She trembled.

"Throw it," Cupid ordered. The men's eyes didn't turn to the little man. All they saw was Rhiannon.

Rhiannon tossed the stick over their heads. They didn't move, merely watched her as the stick landed far behind them. Their eyes narrowed. Weakly, she whispered, "Fetch?"

The men turned from her, taking off at a full run to do as she bid. Rhiannon took a deep breath, relieved that they headed away from her.

"See." the troll declared. He did a little jig in his humor, watching the men run around like trained mongrels. "They don't hate you. They worship you. Worship you like a goddess."

Rhiannon swallowed, suddenly growing nervous at the troll's smile that curled from ear to ear. He enjoyed this way too much and didn't look as if he had any intention of leaving the castle. Her mouth opened as she started to speak but then she heard a noise.

Turning to the men, she saw them fighting over the stick. One man punched the other as he tried to grab it. As the man rolled from the blow, his body shifted into a wolf form and he came up on all fours. Instantly, the other two shifted as well, snarling, snapping, biting. She flinched as the smallest lycan was caught up in the largest one's jaws.

"Can't you stop them?" Rhiannon asked, not wanting to be the cause of a brawl. She looked for the troll. To her horror, she saw that he was gone.

She heard a growl and turned to watch the fight. Two wolves lay unmoving on the ground. The third and largest lycan guard was coming for her, his massive paws hitting the ground in heavy thuds. Rhiannon screamed, backing away. Her back hit upon the battlements. She was trapped.

The wolf tossed the stick from his mouth to her feet, barking, snapping his hideously frightening jaw at her. His eyes were shifted to yellow, eerie as they looked her over. The fur along his spine stood on end, waiting for her movement of approval.

Rhiannon didn't know what the lycan wanted from her. She gasped weakly for air. Tears streamed down her face. She clutched desperately to the stone wall as she looked for her guide. The troll was nowhere to be found.

His chest heaving, the lycan edged closer. Rhiannon closed her eyes tight, bracing herself for the impact of the wolf's bite. A nose nudged into her thighs. She whimpered, chewing her lips to keep from screaming.

The wolf inhaled deeply, as it panted hot, steamy breaths into her thighs. His throat rumbled in pleasure, almost euphoric. He tried to bury his nose deeper into her, edging her thighs apart so that he could rub intimately into her.

"Ilar," Rhiannon whimpered, automatically wishing he was there to save her. Why did she have to listen to the smelly little troll? She struck her hand into the wolf's head, knocking him from between her legs.

The wolf growled in loud outrage. She tried to run. He snapped at her, his teeth biting into her gown. The material tore as she fell.

Ilar's eyes narrowed. He stopped speaking in mid-sentence, hearing a familiar voice crying out his name. Without thought, he shifted, flesh molding into a dark brown coat, as he took off across the yard on all fours. His dark blue tunic fell from his body as he moved. Malak, not to be left out of the fray, was right behind him clad only in his raven black fur.

"Ilar," Rhiannon shouted. He followed the sound, picking up her scent as he raced across the yard.

Eyes turned to follow the wolves as they moved. Larus held up his hand, keeping the others at bay as he alone ran after them. The king stayed in his human form, jogging several paces behind to assess the situation.

Ilar's eyes narrowed to see the lycan pawing at Rhiannon's dress, ripping it as he tried to strip her from her clothes. She was on her stomach, her fingers clawing at the dirt as she tried to escape. Lunging forward, Ilar dug his paws into the wolf's side, knocking him over. They squared off, growling.

Rhiannon gasped as the weight was thrust from her body. Scurrying to her hands and knees, she crawled away from the fighting wolves. Suddenly, she stopped, seeing two black paws blocking her path. She jumped back, but to her surprise, the wolf didn't attack her. Its golden eyes narrowed and his head lowered as he came forward, sniffing at her lightly. She gasped, her arms lifting weakly to push him back.

Malak sniffed the woman, detecting what it was that made her so irresistible. Seeing her fear, he affectionately licked the side of her face. She jolted in surprise. Malak grinned. No doubt, Ilar wouldn't be too pleased by his affectionate play. The thought only spurred his mischievous self on.

Rhiannon felt the black wolf nudging and licking her, his tail wagging for attention. Absently, she petted him as she realized he meant no harm. She looked at the fray. The two wolves snapped at each other, growling and barking. Without warning, her attacker ran off, snarling and growling even as he retreated.

Seeing the dark brown wolf turning to her, she hugged the friendly black one around the neck, burrowing behind the protective fold of its warm body. She dug her hands into his fur coat, clutching it to her chest in her nervousness. The dark brown wolf's golden eyes shifted to a familiar devilish brown. Rhiannon squeezed tighter to her companion, as Ilar's skin cleared before her. His long locks again grew free down his tanned back and shoulders. The power of him amazed her as his body shifted. Before her eyes, he changed and molded into his naked human form.

Ilar's gaze found her, staring hard at her from his hands and knees as she hugged the wolf's head tighter. His gaze lit with challenge and he bellowed, "Malak."

Rhiannon stiffened to feel a shaking beneath her hands.

"What? She's the one holding me," came a muffled voice pretending innocence.

Rhiannon gasped, feeling the stifled words as they were spoken directly into her breasts. She let go of the wolf, throwing her hands back and up, only to discover that it was a naked man she patted and pressed to her chest. She'd been stroking her hands over the hair falling down his back.

Malak didn't instantly back away. His green eyes lit with mischief. He gave Rhiannon the most audacious grin she'd ever seen and nudged his head into her again, clucking her gently on the chin.

"You must be Lady Rhiannon," Malak murmured. Rhiannon's cheeks turned bright pink. He glanced to her breasts and said with a sultry groan, "It's very nice to meet you, my lady."

Rhiannon fell back, her hands lifting helplessly higher, trembling as if she would push him away only to stop in confusion. All she managed was a feeble, "Uh-huh."

"Malak," Ilar demanded in dark warning, a low growl sounding in the back of his throat. Malak seemed unconcerned.

"Malak. Ilar." The men turned as Larus threw their tunics at them from a distance. He stood by the two fallen wolves. Below in the prisons, the affected lycan guards howled into the mind link, hitting their bodies upon the bars as they tried to get free. Angrily, the king demanded, "Stop fooling around."

Malak winked audaciously at Rhiannon as he backed away on all fours. Rhiannon watched them all, helpless. She made a weak noise and didn't move.

Ilar shot to his feet, catching his tunic with one hand. He glared down at her and Rhiannon trembled, covering her bared legs the best she could with the torn skirt of her gown. Ilar whipped his tunic around his body. Malak did the same, only more leisurely. Rhiannon did her best not to look at either of the naked men. Not that her modesty mattered, as they appeared comfortable with her seeing them in all their glory.

"What are you doing out?" Ilar asked, looking down at her. "I ordered you to stay inside."

"Little man," she stuttered, trying to point where she last saw the troll.

Ilar's look cut her off. He eyed her as if she were insane. She trembled, gesturing weakly in confusion.

In their language so the mortal couldn't understand him, Larus turned to Ilar, and ordered, "Two of our men are fallen because of this temptress and the others are thrashing themselves bloody against their prison bars. I don't care what it is that brought her here. You get up to your bedchamber and mate with her. I'll have no more of this. Even if it isn't the way to break the enchantment, I think we have little choice at this time but to try."

Ilar's eyes lit with fire as he looked over to Rhiannon. She stared at them, frightened.

Malak grinned sheepishly. "I think you should go mate with her, Ilar. It's the only way to end this cruel jest."

Larus and Ilar studied him at the words.

Larus frowned. He could get the barest hint of the mortal's scent as it tried to stir into his blood. He kept upwind of her. "You are unmated, Malak, yet you are not affected by her?"

Malak's grin widened. Looking over at Rhiannon, he chuckled. "No, but she is beautiful enough to stir my blood. If you command me, I'll gladly take her to my bed."

Ilar growled in low warning. Malak held up his hands, still chuckling.

"However," Malak continued, seeing he pushed Ilar too far. "The enchanted scent she carries is one I am immune to."

"You know what it is?" Ilar demanded.

"Yes, I know," Malak mused, drawing out his suspense with deviant pleasure. His eyes narrowed as he stared at Ilar.

"By all the lycan, Malak." Larus thundered, past the point of breaking. He wanted the howling in his head to stop. "Out with it."

"You didn't, perhaps, happen to insult a troll, did you?" Malak asked, pointedly staring at Ilar.

"What? Are you saying a troll did this to her?" Ilar said, skeptical.

"Yes, it's a troll's philter that's clouding her head," Malak said, laughing. To him the situation was hilarious. "It's nothing more than an abundance of pure pheromone. It's why the unmated males of Lycaon are insane. I bested a troll once in sport and did get immunity to all troll magic. It was either that or his eldest daughter for a prize. Until now, I've never had a need for it."

Larus's expression fell, and he grimaced. "Cupid."

Ilar frowned, remembering how he teased the smelly little varmint one night after drinking too much. The troll had been absolutely vile and refused to bathe. He kept popping back up, too, after they'd thrown him out a dozen times. Sheepishly, he said, "Yes, Cupid. I might have called him a rosy-faced cherub."

Malak's laughter only grew. Rhiannon watched in wonder, not knowing what they said in their growling speech. They weren't paying attention to her, and she slowly edged to her feet.

"It's you who insulted him, Ilar, so it's you who must get him to lift this wretched curse," Larus commanded with a growl of exasperation. "All this fuss over an insulted troll. Malak, you go with him to find Cupid. Make sure the little troll sees reason and make sure Ilar doesn't anger him further. Ilar, hold off on mating until we know for sure that it will end this. I won't have the enchantment becoming worse if the others grow to be jealous of your claim to her. Who knows what Cupid had in mind when he did this?"

Ilar and Malak both nodded in understanding. Suddenly, Larus frowned. Rhiannon was making a run for it. Jerking his thumb, the king huffed in exasperation,

"But first, Ilar, get her back in your chambers before more of her damned scent is brandished about."

Malak's chuckling only grew as Ilar took off at a sprint to catch up to Rhiannon. Malak glanced at Larus. The king winked at him.

"Yes, I know," Malak said, waving the man away only to follow behind him as they each lifted an unconscious soldier over their shoulders. The lycans weren't severely injured. They'd be sore, but they would live. The king led the way down to the prisons. "However, I'm not going to be the one to tell him there's more between him and a human than the curse. Let him discover that one for himself."

RHIANNON HEARD HEAVY FOOTFALLS BEHIND HER. She let loose a squeal. Her bare feet pumped faster until her lungs nearly exploded with her effort to be free. The breeze whipped over her bare legs, coming through the part in her ripped gown. She didn't care. All she knew was that she wanted to be free of this strange place.

Seeing a side gate, Rhiannon ran for it. She tried to squeeze her body through the bars. It was too small, but it didn't stop her from fitting her head through in an effort to get out.

Ilar chuckled as he caught her. With a sigh, he dipped his hand into the iron bars and gently forced her head back inside. Rhiannon groaned at being captured and instantly moved to strike him.

Ilar caught her hand in his. Knowing it was only a

troll's revenge that brought her to him, he relaxed. Trolls were very powerful, but they had no allegiance to mortals and only used their magic for self-gain or mischief. They wouldn't open the portals to humankind, so that the mortals may flood into their world.

Naturally, when word spread of this trickery, Cupid would be in serious trouble with the other races. He risked too much for revenge. But, then, trolls weren't known for their concern of consequences either.

Rhiannon swung her other hand at him and Ilar caught that one just as easily. Smiling, he saw a rip revealed part of her cleavage to his eyes. His body lit with fire. She glared at him, her eyes hot and murderous.

"Let me go," Rhiannon said, fighting him. Her teeth snapped at his wrist, trying to bite him. He artfully pulled her head into the warm, protective fold of his chest. He held her tight. Her words were muffled by hard muscle, as she tried to scream, "I want to go home. You're all crazy."

"Shh," Ilar soothed, trying to lead her back to the castle. She jerked in his arms, clawing and scratching violently to be free. He let her go, though her fighting didn't hurt him. If anything, he was more aroused.

"Do not tell me to be quiet." she cried. "I tell you there was a little man who brought me here. He hit me over the head and brought me here. And he was in your bedchamber and he smelled vile. That's who you seek. Go and find him. I'm through with all of this. I'm going home."

"How will you get there?" Ilar asked, with infinite patience. His eyes devoured her legs, knowing that soon he would be able to stake claim to her. The danger had passed and Malak said the only way he knew to end her enchantment was to mate with her. Ilar licked his lips.

"I'll walk." She tried to storm past him, making her way back into the bailey yard.

"Rhian," Ilar said, reaching his hand to stop her. He grabbed her and pulled her back. "It's not safe yet. We need to get you inside."

"Not safe?" she asked, disbelieving. "What is wrong with you beasts? I think I'll be much safer out there in the wilderness than locked in here with you."

"Cupid has put an enchantment on you," Ilar explained. "It makes our kind crazy. Once the enchantment is gone, the threat will be gone."

"What are you saying?" Rhiannon shook, torn between anger and desire. Oh, but he was handsome to behold. She stung with embarrassment from their last meeting. Even seeing his body shift from wolf to man couldn't lessen her longing for him. If anything, it made it worse. Oh, she was a wicked, wicked woman.

"You are under a... a love spell. That is why they

attack you. They seek to mate with you. Once the spell is gone, the attraction will end. Now, please Rhian, come inside where it's safe." Ilar kept his voice gentle. "If I let you beyond these walls, they will hunt you in the forest. You have no choice in this. If you wish to live, you will follow me."

Rhiannon's eyes moistened slightly with tears as she looked at him, reading the truth in his eyes. He'd only kissed her because of a spell. He didn't truly want her. Taking a hasty step toward the castle, she walked, keeping a furious pace so that he only saw her back. She wouldn't let him see her pain at his admission. When they reached the stairwell leading to his tower, she asked softly, "You know how to end this enchantment?"

Ilar looked over her body, staring boldly at her hips. They swayed back and forth before his vision, a hypnotic seduction to his senses. "Yes, I think I do. Malak, ah, he is the man you—"

"Ah-ha, yes, I know," she hastened, not wanting to think of the naked man she'd pressed firmly to her chest. The memory only mortified her.

"Malak and I will go to find Cupid. We'll confirm that he's the cause of this curse and see if he cannot lift it from you."

Rhiannon reached his door and pushed it open. Wearily, she walked inside. She kept her back to him, going to the window to stare out of the narrow slit. She didn't turn to him, refusing to let him see the tears that streamed down her cheeks.

"Rhian, I must have your promise that you will stay in here until I get back." He reached to touch her shoulder lightly. She shivered, and he assumed she was still shaken from her experience in the bailey yard. Ilar didn't want to think what would have happened to her if he'd not heard her cry.

"You have it," she answered, having no wish to be attacked again. He ran his fingers down her arm and she knew he only touched her because of the enchantment. "And I'll remind you of yours, Ilar. Now that the danger is passing, you will bring me home."

"I never promised to bring you home," he said. "I only promised to protect you."

Her jaw rose, and she pulled away.

"But, if it's what you wish, I'll find a way to bring you home, Rhian. I promise."

"Thank you," she said. "It is what I wish."

Ilar paused, watching the back of her head. The others still howled in agony and he knew he had to find Cupid to end it. But he didn't want to leave her.

"I'll send you food and a new gown," he said, before walking out the door.

Rhiannon didn't move until she heard the key hitting

in the latch to lock her in. Tears poured from her eyes, blinding her with a sob. She gripped the hard stone, falling down the side of the wall. She hit the stone floor in misery. Ilar only wanted her because of a spell and all she could think to do was weep.

18

"You should have seen her." Cupid sighed with longing, as he looked across the campfire to the other trolls. Their small eyes stared back at him, reflecting the fire like miniature fireflies. Their wrinkled skin looked much like Cupid's though their noses were smaller and their ears perhaps a bit larger. "She was the loveliest mortal I've ever seen."

Cupid closed his eyes dreamily, knowing he had the others' rapt attention as he spoke of his beloved temptress.

"Agrona," Cupid moaned, stopping to light his long, gnarled pipe with a burning stick from the campfire. "Agrona, the name of legends. She has the loveliest three hairs growing out of her mole. Ah, so perfect, my temptress, my swamp bottom vision of toadstool exquisiteness. I'll be going back for her."

"Three," a pudgy troll grunted. His face looked as if someone had squished it down and together. His nose folded up over his lips. He nodded thoughtfully. "It's a lucky count for hairs on a mole."

"Bah." another, longer troll returned. His dirty brown pants stank to high heaven, much to his companions' envy. "I think six is a sight more attractive."

Malak and Ilar glanced at each other, rolling their eyes. It hadn't taken long for them to sniff out Cupid's location. The odor he and his fellow trolls emitted leaked downwind for leagues. By the time they reached the little campfire it was well into the evening.

The lycans saw through the darkness as if it was daylight. Their eyes flashed with golden slivers. The moon was half full, shining the most exquisite silver over the land. The giant orb would shift its colors with the magic of seasons, but the silver moon always lasted the longest.

Cupid was lost in daydreams of his mortal goddess when the shadows of Malak and Ilar fell over him. The other trolls gasped, running to hide as the two lycan men stood behind Cupid.

"Where...?" Cupid began, not finished talking about

his temptress. He was about to tell them about her one eyebrow and her pustules.

"Cupid," Ilar stated, his displeasure evident.

Cupid squealed like a pig, jumping to his feet to run away. Ilar tilted his head to Malak. Malak leapt into the air, landing gracefully before the troll. Cupid whined, sitting back, his dirty bottom thumping onto the ground. Taking the pipe from his mouth, he grumbled, "What is it you want, lycan? This is a private fire. No room for you to sit."

"You know why I'm here." Ilar narrowed his eyes as he studied the offensive little man.

"Do I now?" Cupid grumbled. Taking his pipe, he poked it into the air. "I suppose you'd be wantin' to apologize for insulting me. Well, I have no use for your apologies. Begone, lycan."

"*Cupid!*" Ilar's voice lowered into a growl.

"Oh, very well." Unexpectedly, a wide grin formed on the troll's long lips. Gloating, he said, "It is I that set the mortal in your midst. It is I who enchanted all of Lycaon. And it is I who have proven my magical worth. Never shall you doubt me again, Lord Ilar."

"End it," Ilar commanded, his tone darkening. Malak stood quietly, listening.

"I cannot end it," Cupid beamed, smoking on his pipe, very pleased with himself.

Ilar leaned over and lifted him off the ground by the back of his neck. Cupid grunted in surprise. His little legs pumped in the air as he tried to get free and his pipe fell to the ground, cracking.

Yelling in protest, Cupid said, "Only you can end it. You, Ilar, must mate yourself to the mortal woman. That's how the curse goes away. Now, set me down before I take offense. You do not want to be upsettin' me again, lycan."

Ilar growled for effect and set the troll back down. Instantly, he knew that the little varmint spoke the truth. He detected it just beneath his foul odor. Turning, he motioned his head toward Malak. His friend leapt back over the fire to follow him.

"Ha," Cupid yelled behind them. The other trolls crawled out of hiding, coming from under mossy leaves and rotted tree bark. "I have my revenge, lycan. You will mate the ugly mortal or your kind will suffer."

The other trolls cackled in pleasure at Cupid's cunning, taking their seats back around the campfire. Cupid kept a wary ear pricked in Ilar's direction, as he continued with this narrative of womanly perfection.

Ilar and Malak walked from the troll campsite in silence. When the trolls were out of earshot, Malak grinned into the night. Ilar returned the look with a heated one of his own.

"Yes, Lord Ilar, you will have to mate the ugly mortal," Malak said, teasing.

Ilar's eyes lit with passion. "Yes. That I most certainly will. Duty demands it."

Their bodies shifted into lycan form. Before turning to run, they grabbed their tunics between their teeth. Then, tearing along the countryside at a full sprint, the two wolves raced back to Lycaon.

19

IT WAS LATE WHEN ILAR MADE IT BACK TO LYCAON. He stopped to bathe the travel dust from his body in the stream, wanting to go to Rhiannon fresh. As they entered the castle, Malak, knowing his friend's eagerness to tend to his duty, offered to go to Larus and explain what they had learned.

Ilar took the tower steps two at a time. A grin spread over his features. He couldn't help it. His body sung with sweet anticipation. Rhiannon's face danced within his brain, tempting him, teasing him, beckoning him. Her lips haunted his mouth and the intimate feel of her moist fire still burned into his hand. This time there would be no stopping. He would have her.

He trembled as he reached into his tunic for the key.

Unlocking the door, he crept inside, his eyes going first to the bed. Frowning, he saw she wasn't there.

"Rhian?" he called, stepping forward, his heart twisting in panic. A soft moan sounded on the floor and he was again able to smile. She was a stubborn one. He'd give her that.

Coming forward, he saw her before the fireplace, wrapped in the blanket he'd thrown down there the night before. He never expected she'd sleep there again, especially since he hadn't been in the bed. Ilar frowned. He wondered if that meant she still wanted nothing to do with his bed. Her body readily melted for him, but what of her mind? Did her mind still resist him? Did she still think him nothing more than a hideous beast unworthy of touching her?

A whimper left her parted lips, and she turned, uncomfortable. He slowly lowered himself to kneel beside her. He cupped beneath her shoulders and legs, lifting her into his arms. She jolted slightly in surprise but didn't waken, as she nestled into the warmth of his chest. A soft moan left her parted lips.

Ilar smiled slightly. She was always so chilled compared to him, so fragile and light. It made him want to protect her even more. It made him want to warm her.

Ilar laid her gently on the bed. Rhiannon sighed in her sleep, snuggling into the soft mattress. When he pulled back, a small sound of protest left her throat and her hand stirred lazily in his direction.

For a moment, he looked at her. He lifted his hand, moving over her sleep-flushed cheek in a tender caress. He wanted this. He wanted it badly. It was his duty to seduce her. But he hesitated, wondering if it was what she would want if he left it to her to decide her fate.

The fairies had brought her a new gown. This one was of a soft blue. Her cheeks were rosy, giving the feeling of comfort to her sleeping features. Her curls, so glorious to behold and so soft to touch, strung haphazardly all around her face.

Ilar kept his eyes steadily on her, as he slowly went around the bed. Stripping from his clothes, he let them fall onto the floor as he crawled next to her.

"Rhian," he said to her still face. Her breath came in even draws. Lowering for a kiss, he whispered to her mouth, "Rhian, wake up."

This time she moaned louder. Ilar's lips brushed against hers. He held her jaw, tilting her lips to better fit against his.

Rhiannon blinked, feeling as if she were in a dream. Ilar traced her mouth with his tongue, parting her lips to him. She moaned again, coming more fully awake at the sensations coursing throughout her body. She lifted her hand from the mattress, tangling her fingers into his dampened hair.

"Ilar?" she sighed, her voice still rough with sleep. Her knee rose to meet his hip, the gown keeping her from tossing the limb over him. His roaming hands did delightful things to her senses. His touch appeared to be everywhere at once. She made soft sounds in the back of her throat, whimpering ever so lightly as he continued his kisses. She twined her fingers into his long hair as she pressed along his arm, feeling his strength.

Ilar groaned at her willingness. He deepened his kiss, growing more demanding as he tried to consume her with his need.

"Take off your gown," he murmured, already reaching his hands to pull up her skirt.

Rhiannon made a soft noise, feeling the air stir by her thighs. When he had her legs bared, his arm scooped under her waist to lift her. With a deft move that left her breathless, he pulled the gown over her head. Rhiannon gasped in awe of his quick strength and supernatural speed.

Ilar laid her back down. A devilishly handsome grin curled on his mouth, as he looked deep into her eyes. "Much better. Now I can feel all of you."

He stroked his fingers down her throat, moving them over her flesh. Ilar watched her response and let her see his. Dipping to taste a breast, he brought his body down to brush longingly against hers. He lapped at the creamy texture of her skin, loving her soft, fragile feel against his lips.

Rhiannon ran her fingers along his muscles, learning the feel of his greater strength, liking the way his body moved and flexed beneath her palms. His touch was addictive and his masculine body even more so. She wanted to explore all of him, every hot inch.

Rhiannon knew this might be her last chance to be with him. Soon he'd be taking her back to her world—a world that seemed so dismal and gray. Right here in his arms, for the first time in her life, everything felt so vivid, so real, so wonderful. But, what else could she do? She couldn't stay here. Ilar wouldn't want her to stay once the enchantment was broken.

Rhiannon pushed at his shoulder and Ilar thought she meant to push him off her breast, where he found great delight. He moaned his denial, parting from her only long enough to pull her other nipple into a hard, matching peak. He gripped her waist, kneading insistently into her flesh.

"I can't," she gasped, breathless. His mouth became more insistent, almost fierce. Pleasure shot all over her body from her breast. She arched, pushing herself more fully against him. "Ilar…"

His eyes were dark when he pulled back. He took in her impassioned face, devouring her with his intense look. He worked his hand, clenching and unclenching it over her hipbone. "Do not deny us both, Rhian. I only mean to give you pleasure."

Rhiannon blushed at the heated fire in his words. Her eyes dipped down, shy. "You're lying on my hand. I cannot reach."

Ilar grinned, lifting his hips slightly. Rhiannon pulled her hand from under him. When he didn't resume kissing her, she moved to touch his chest, peeking up at him for approval. His eyes closed and his breath deepened as she skimmed his nipples. His hands found her newly freed fingers, and he drew them onto his arousal. He'd dreamed of her touch, longed for it there against his solid heat.

Rhiannon was surprised at how hard, yet silky smooth, his shaft really was. His body jerked slightly as she moved her hand against him. Not sure what she was supposed to do with his erection, she merely squeezed, slowly exploring its length. She rubbed her leg onto his, spurring his fingers to glide along her hips. She kissed his chest as he had hers, licking at him, discovering the taste of his flesh. Ilar groaned, liking the gentle, teasing feel of her lips. His body lurched. It was almost too much.

"Ilar?" she pleaded. He moved to look at her and

she became embarrassed, trying to burrow into his chest so he couldn't see her face. "Could... would you...?"

She bit her lip, turning red.

He grinned. The look was altogether roguish and handsome. He trailed his hand along the inside of her leg. He maneuvered himself above her with a deft lift of his hips. Rhiannon gasped, blinking in surprise. He used his legs to part hers.

"You want me to touch you?" he murmured, nuzzling her throat.

"*Mm,*" she sighed in agreement, too weak to lay voice to the plea. She felt as if he was everywhere at once, causing havoc inside her, making her blood race. His delightfully hard body rubbed into hers. His flesh was like formed metal. His touch was so vigorous, so compelling and strong—from the brush of his hair-roughened thighs to her soft ones, the press of his rigid abdomen to her yielding waist.

Ilar let his erection fall heavy onto her hip. Rhiannon jolted, feeling the fire of it heating her with a new kind of excitement. It was fear, apprehension, longing, anticipation—so many things that she couldn't stop to consider, only feel.

Slowly, he stroked himself against her, readying his hips for the first conquering thrust. Ever since meeting her, his shaft had been hard and aware, waiting for this moment when she was ready to take him in.

Ilar rose up and guided his shaft to her slick opening, stroking the tip along her folds. He heard her heart pounding in her chest, smelled the sweet calling of her body's desire. A growl of intense pleasure left his throat.

Rhiannon blinked in surprise when it wasn't his hands that intimately found her. He urged her to open to him, stroking harder and deeper with each pass, gliding along the sensitive nub of her flesh from top arch to the cleft of her backside. She arched, panting in delight to discover the pleasure of his wicked heat against her. She shivered.

Ilar moved to her ear, whispering, "Is this where you want me to touch you?"

"Yes." She opened herself up to him at his hand's insistence, trusting, waiting.

Ilar gradually slid himself forward. Straining for control, he kept from mindlessly thrusting. Oh, but she was tight, gripping his thick length almost painfully.

Rhiannon gasped at the white fire searing through her, but soon the pleasure of his touch overshadowed the ache. The sound didn't stop him as he glided deeper, forging her to his body, marking her as his.

Ilar mindlessly pushed past the boundary of her

innocence, liking that no other had dared to lay claim to her.

"You feel so warm," Ilar asserted. He drew back, only to force himself in harder. Rhiannon's eyes widened, surprised to feel a strange friction at the movement. She watched his face tense as he continued, "So moist."

A need grew inside where he touched her, replacing the dull pain. Her heartbeat pounded in her chest, thumping as if the organ would free itself. His stroke was slow, sure, hitting deeper with each pass until he'd forced his length fully into her. It hurt, but the pain felt strangely wonderful. She didn't want it to stop. Her hips moved, meeting him at each thrust.

Ilar could take no more of this slow torture. He groaned. His eyes changed to a scintillating golden fire, as he lifted his body. His hips pumped, vigorous and strong. When she did not protest, he did it again.

Rhiannon was stunned by the sudden change in his lovemaking. She grew excited, feeling his power overtaking them. He found her breast, demanding and confident as a thumb circled over the tip, pinching ever so slightly. His lips captured hers, moaning his passion into her body as she breathed him in.

She tensed, straining against him, reaching and searching for what he gave. She was almost there, almost at the point, almost...

Suddenly, he stiffened, an untamed cry of ecstasy leaving his lips as he met the violence of his release. Ilar fell against her heated skin, panting for breath. His teeth lazily grazed her flesh as he drew them over her racing pulse. Rhiannon's eyes widened in wonder.

"It was... different," she mumbled.

Ilar lifted to study her, frowning.

"What?" she demanded, growing defensive at his look. "It was... pleasant enough. But I don't see what everyone goes on about."

"Different?" His eyes narrowed, knowing she teased him. He also knew his body came too fast, knew she wasn't near the point he could push her. "I'll show you different, Rhian."

Before she knew what he was up to, he had her hands lifted above her head and pinned beneath a strong hand. Drawing his fingers down her stomach, he stared deeply into her eyes, forcing her to watch him. Leisurely, he tweaked the swollen nub guarding her entrance. She jerked. He smiled wickedly.

"Ah," she gasped when he did it again.

Ilar had met the burning need her enchantment wrought and, now that his desire was somewhat sated, he could concentrate on her body's demands. Already he felt his shaft stirring to claim again, rising to her challenge. Her wrists pulled, but he held them with his superior strength. He stroked, growing bold as he again heated a fire beneath his touch. His mouth kissed her breasts, exploring her arms and chest, tasting of her neck and lips.

Rhiannon's head rocked back and forth, rolling in the golden bed of curls. By the time his fingers finished their teasing caresses she was parting her legs and begging him to come inside. His name left her lips on endless pants, calling to him.

Ilar lifted over her once more, his body straining as he moved. She loved the look of his muscled form. He guided himself to her, dipping shallowly into her moist entrance.

"Ilar, please," she begged. "Oh, please, don't..."

Still he held back, torturing her, making her ride her emotions to the brink of insanity and longing. Rhiannon was mindless in her search for him, her mouth opening wide as she bit at the air. The sweat from her skin allowed a wrist to slide free and her fingers burst forward. She pushed hard into his chest, digging her nails roughly into his flesh.

Taken by surprise, he groaned against the pleasure her clawing fingernails brought forth in his body. His grip loosened to free her. She forced him over onto his back.

Rhiannon sat astride him. Licking her lips, she liked

the newfound power the position afforded her. She let her fingers roam over his chiseled body, scratching lightly.

With much care, she angled her hips trying to get him inside her. First, he slipped back, gliding intimately along her backside, spreading her cheeks. She jolted. That was a new pleasure altogether. Then, his shaft slipped forward running along her swollen clit. Rhiannon groaned in frustration and bucked her hips against him.

Ilar chuckled as he watched her. He purposefully moved off course to frustrate her further.

"Ilar," she moaned. "Help me."

"Like this," he murmured, taking pity on her suffering as his hands rose to her hips. He guided himself into her, letting her control the depth.

Rhiannon groaned as he stretched her again. The throaty sound echoed in his head and he couldn't help controlling her thrusts as he taught her how to ride him. He gripped her with his hands, lifting her hips high only to let her weight bring her slowly back down.

It was so much easier this time. The ache was still there, but it was nothing compared to the gratification of his body in hers. Maybe it was the enchantment that made her forget it, or perhaps it was the intuitive way she knew he was meant to be inside her like this.

"Ah, let me," she demanded. She dug her hands into him as she took over, fighting his control over her hips until he was forced to release her.

Ilar's stomach tensed, delighting as she quickened her pace. To his amazement, she became as wild as he'd been as she sought her fulfillment. She began bucking against him, slamming down onto his hips. His hands fell back, crossing behind his head to keep them back. His narrowed eyes watched her, taking in the bouncing show of her breasts. He let her have complete dominance, loving each tempestuous stroke of her tight passage.

"Ilar," she cried, the agony building unbearably inside her. She didn't know how to end it. She clawed at him, rocking his thickness deeper and harder.

"Yes, Rhian, keep going. Keep moving." Ilar knew she neared her peak, felt her hot body quiver. He saw the confusion on her face. "Ah, yes, just like that. Take me deeply within you."

Rhiannon screamed. She jerked as her body convulsed. His hips kept moving beneath her, urging her to keep riding, not to stop. She convulsed again, this time strong and hard. Her body became so tense she couldn't move. She froze, arching above him, overflowing with intense climactic pleasure.

The tremors of her climax pulled him in, urging a response from his body as her depths seized tightly upon his shaft. The erotic sight of her fulfillment burned into his brain. His stomach muscles flexed, nearly causing him to sit up with the force of his release. The seed spilled from his jerking body, shooting out of him into her. His howl of pleasure joined hers. His arms reached forward to hold her against him. Rhiannon nearly fainted as she fell into his embrace, her weight pushing him once more onto the bed.

"Now that," she said. "That was different."

Ilar chuckled. He was completely sated. Pulling her down beside him, he trapped her to his body with a heavy leg.

"The enchantment has ended," he said, nuzzling her ear in contentment.

Rhiannon froze, pulling away from the tease of his breath. Did this mean he was done with her? Did it imply he no longer desired her?

"Then it's time you took me home," she whispered, not knowing what else to say as she pulled away from him. Without stopping to look at his face, she turned her back. She was too hot for the covers, but she pulled them over her anyway. She felt vulnerable. She didn't want him looking at her, not now, not like this—still shaky and weak.

Ilar narrowed his eyes in resentment. How could she think of going home after what they'd experienced?

When all he could think of was keeping her there, in his bed, under his protection? He swallowed, torn. He knew he could force her to him. The bitter taste of her ultimate rejection was hard to endure. Her body might succumb, but the man-beast wasn't good enough for her human heart.

"Yes," he said, turning his back on her, not bothering to cover himself. "I'll take you home, Rhian. A promise is a promise."

Rhiannon bit her lip to keep from crying. The ache in her chest was overwhelming. She had hoped he would beg her to stay.

Dᴜʀɪɴɢ ᴛʜᴇ ɴɪɢʜᴛ, Rʜɪᴀɴɴᴏɴ'ꜱ ʙᴏᴅʏ ɴᴀᴛᴜʀᴀʟʟʏ drifted under the fold of Ilar's arm. Before she was fully aware, her fingers were caressing his stomach, glancing over the tight ridges. Ilar's eyes opened slowly, feeling the touch. He craned his neck to look down at her sleeping face. Her head was on his arm, trapping him beneath a tangle of wild curls.

He waited, watching to see what she would do while also content to hold her and look at her. She glided her fingers over the curve of his navel, only to stop near his hip. He heard her mumble something. A pretty half smile graced her lips.

"Rhian," he said, flexing his arm beneath her head.

She blinked. The smile faded as she yawned. Her gaze softened for a brief moment as she looked at him only to harden. The pleasure melted behind the blank mask. She snatched her hand from his firm waist.

"Oh." She tried to sit up. His arm trapped her head down by her hair. Thinking he woke her to get her off him, she mumbled, "I'm sorry. I was sleeping."

Ilar's eyes narrowed, darkening. He was ready to make love to her again, but it didn't seem she was so willing. Untangling his limbs from her, he sat up. Rhiannon naturally reached for his back, before drawing her fingers away. Instead, she pulled the coverlet to hide her naked chest.

"We will break our fast. There is no reason for you to stay locked up now the enchantment is gone." Ilar stood and strode naked across the chamber. Rhiannon's eyes devoured him with a newfound appreciation. Her body lurched, remembering what he felt like against her, inside her. With a toss of his arm, a blue tunic was wrapped over his body. "Then, we will journey to Fenris with Malak. If I remember correctly, there is a portal near there."

So soon? Rhiannon bit her lip, fighting the sting of moisture in her eyes. Did he mean to be rid of her so soon? She clutched the coverlet as she scrambled to the floor. Finding her blue gown, she shrugged it over her shoulders, doing her best to stay concealed. There was no point. He didn't try to peek.

When she didn't protest, he turned to find her fully dressed. She came around the bed to face him. His eyes dipped over her form, before saying quietly, "I shall find you some boots. It will be a long walk."

Rhiannon nodded, wondering at the displeasure in his voice.

"Come," he said listlessly, leading her from the bedchamber.

Rhiannon shivered, but could only obey. More than anything she wanted to weep the wretchedness from her heart. It would seem the enchantment really was gone.

THE ENCHANTMENT WASN'T GONE. IT WAS LESSENED, but it hadn't entirely faded. Rhiannon stared around the main hall. The soldiers, who she'd learned were put into the prisons while under her spell's influence, stared up at her from the main hall floor. Their heated eyes had lessened in intensity, but they still desired her. Rhiannon tried to eat the bread and meat set before her, but the overbold eyes were beginning to unnerve her.

"Are they normally like this?" Rhiannon asked, leaning naturally closer to Ilar at her side. She brushed near his thigh causing him to tense.

Ilar looked over her head at Malak, frowning.

Malak nodded. He too sensed the disquiet. Turning back to the hall, they saw each pair of unmated eyes was on Rhiannon's every move. It was clear that Ilar had claimed her as his lover. His scent was all over her.

When Ilar didn't answer, Rhiannon looked at his tense face. Realizing she touched him in public, she frowned and drew her hand away. Irritated, she edged closer to the more amiable Malak, and said teasingly, "They don't mean to eat me, do they? This food is bland, but it's truly not so bad as to warrant an attack."

Malak chuckled, drawing the jealous eyes of the men to him. Leaning close to her, he whispered so only Ilar could hear them, "I think they make plans to challenge Lord Ilar for you."

"Why would they do that?" she asked, a puzzled look coming to her features as she looked over the silent hall.

Ilar's frown deepened as Rhiannon turned her back on him. He wasn't the only man who noticed.

Narrowed eyes watched closely, as the soldiers tried to judge what went on between Ilar and the woman. They didn't touch and act as lovers this morning, though the Commander's scent marked her. The soldiers' gazes lit with a faint stirring of hope. They tensed, forgetting their food and the pretense of eating altogether.

"They know he's marked you as his lover," Malak answered with a shrug. Rhiannon turned bright red. She was mortified. Malak noticed but pretended not to.

"Oh, no," Rhiannon said, seeming to understand Ilar's discontent and the hall's unease. "I'm not his lover."

Malak's brow rose slightly at her quick denial. He smelled otherwise, as could the rest of them. He sniffed her again, to be certain. The marking was strong. He glanced around to make sure none of the others detected her comment. The lycans had very sensitive ears. He was relieved to find none stood to challenge for her.

Breathing a little easier, Malak studied the woman's pretty face before looking at his friend. Ilar had tensed in outrage at her words. The Commander's eyes bore into her back in growing fury.

"No," Rhiannon said softly. She colored to a light pink and looked at her hands, not knowing Ilar listened. Under her breath, she explained, "It was to end the enchantment, but I don't think it worked."

Malak's eyes rounded. He glanced over her head to where his friend was gripping his goblet like he wanted nothing more than to beat Lady Rhiannon over the head with it. He tried to catch his attention, but Ilar was too lost in his anger to heed Malak's silent warning.

"Lord Ilar," King Larus said, coming up the table to join them. He glanced around the hall at the abnormally silent men. The mind link was the quietest it had been since Lady Rhiannon's arrival, but it still murmured with grumbles and grunts. It would only take one provocation to get them howling again.

Ilar lowered his goblet to the table and turned to the king. Rhiannon blinked at the sound, turning to glance at who spoke. Ilar's back was to her. A slow smile came to Malak's lips.

"I think you should go find Cupid on your way to Fenris," the king said so that Rhiannon couldn't understand his words. "The spell has worn thin, but it hasn't gone away."

"Perhaps it takes time," Malak said.

"No," Larus said. "Enchantments may build and grow, but once they are broken, they should be broken. It would seem Cupid's revenge isn't yet complete. Go to him and try to discover what he has planned. It's wise you take her back to the mortal realm—that is, if you don't wish to keep her for yourself?"

Malak met the king's gaze, exchanging a knowing look.

Ilar denied him instantly with a shake of his head. No, Rhiannon made it clear she wanted to go home and he would keep his word and take her.

"No?" Larus inquired, before adding, "Then, it is wise to bring her back. Unless she's under a man's protection, she cannot survive in our land. We have taken her in, so it is up to us to make sure she remains safe. I don't wish to have an unmated human running around."

Rhiannon knew they talked about her. Her cheeks flamed slightly in irritation as they refused to let her understand their words.

"Yes," Malak answered when Ilar didn't. "We will find that troll easily enough on our way to Fenris. By the looks of these men, we should be going."

"I agree," Larus said.

Rhiannon blinked as Malak and Ilar both stood abruptly from the table. Malak motioned for her to come. Ilar turned his back and said nothing. Taking a quick drink, she moved to follow the men.

THE FRONT GATES OF LYCAON FADED INTO nothingness as they walked in silence. Ilar and Malak each carried a pack slung over their shoulders. The thick forest of red trees broke open to a long field of rolling grasses. The sun shone brightly in the soft purple sky. Rhiannon's gaze stayed down, looking for snakes hidden within the field. She'd bound the sides of her hair back from her face, but the wind still whipped the long curls over her back.

They walked at a slow pace. She was glad for the fresh air and for the boots Ilar had managed to acquire for her. They were comfortable, if not a little worn. Her legs jerked. She felt like running with her arms widespread. She held back, not wanting to disrupt the pace Ilar and Malak set.

Malak, frowning, used the mind link to ask Ilar, *'Shouldn't we shift and carry her upon our backs? It would be faster. At this rate, it will take us a sennight to get to Fenris.'*

Answering with a growl, Ilar said, *'No, let her walk. I have no wish to carry her.'*

Rhiannon heard a snort and looked up. The silent duo made for dull traveling companions. For a while, she passed the time humming every song she could remember in her head. Once, when the tune got away from her and she hummed out loud, Ilar's look stopped her.

Hours passed and the field gradually thinned as they neared a rocky path wide enough for all three to walk side by side. The rolling field turned into small hills. The low hills grew into larger foothills. And, as the day turned into evening, the foothills finally rose in the distance to show a range of mountains.

Rhiannon tried to pause in awe to look at the splendor of the landscape, never having seen such a sight. Ilar's hand on her arm pulling her forward kept her moving. She shot him a glare that he didn't seem to notice.

Rhiannon sighed, seeing the shadowing of a silver moon on the evening sky. If she ever saw that little troll again, she'd give him what for.

Sighing, she ignored Ilar, who for some reason appeared to be in the blackest of all their moods. She turned to Malak. The man glanced down at her open attention. He really was a tall man, and she felt dwarfed between the two lycans. Casually, she asked the lycan, "Are you married, Lord Malak?"

Malak blinked in surprise at the forward question. Ilar's eyes darkened over her head to glare at his friend in unconcealed jealousy. Malak answered her expectant smile, "No, my lady."

Ilar growled. Rhiannon was flirting with Malak. And right in front of him. To inquire such of a man's mated status was to hint that you wanted him as your lover. She didn't even try to hide her blatant advances from him. She wasn't even marked as his woman for a day. It was beyond insulting that she would seek another so quickly.

"Oh, then do you rule Fenris alone?" she inquired, wanting to keep the conversation going. At least it would take her mind from the endless miles stretching ahead of them—and the dark looks the moody Ilar kept giving her. She had half a mind to tell him to go back, that she'd find her own way. However, she couldn't do it. Even if he didn't want to be there, she desperately wanted him with her—even distant and irritable as he was. Her whole body had stayed focused on him in one way or another.

"Yes," Malak answered carefully.

Ilar snorted. Rhiannon blinked, turning to study him. Now what was wrong with him? It's not like he was talking to her.

Keeping her eyes steadily on Ilar, she asked Malak, "And is Fenris far from here, Lord Malak?"

"Well, no, usually we can make the run in little over a day," the lycan answered.

"Ah, are we close, then?" Rhiannon asked, blinking. She'd thought they would be sleeping outside by the looks of the satchels.

"No, not so close," Malak answered, grinning. "We usually shift to run. At this pace we'll be there in maybe a half a sennight's time."

"I can run," Rhiannon said, embarrassed that she was the reason they moved so slow. "Maybe, not as fast as you, but I can run."

Ilar snorted. This time it was louder. Rhiannon stopped, placing her hands on her hips and refusing to walk another step as she stared at Ilar's back. Malak grinned, not turning. It had taken him a while, but he realized Rhiannon only spoke to him to irritate Ilar. It worked better than she realized. Ilar and Malak stopped, turning to look at her in expectation.

When she didn't move, only continued to glare at Ilar, Malak said, "We should camp here tonight. I think there's a small pool up ahead with fish. Ilar, if you would start a fire, I'll get our supper."

Ilar knew Malak was purposefully leaving them alone. He barely turned to acknowledge him as he left.

Aside from Ilar handing her a piece of dried meat back at the field, Rhiannon hadn't eaten and her stomach turned at the idea of supper, making her even more irritable toward Ilar. Unable to bite her tongue, she told him, "Why don't you go away."

"Why?" he demanded, stalking forward to tower over her. "So you can be alone with Malak?"

Rhiannon blinked, surprised by the accusations. "At least he'll look at me and talk to me. It's more than you have done all day. If you're so miserable, leave. I'll find my own way to Fenris and the portal. I don't need you."

"I promised to protect you and I'll protect you," Ilar said. Truthfully, he didn't want to leave her alone with Malak. He'd seen the way she smiled at his friend. She didn't look at him in such a way. It tore at his insides. What he wouldn't give for one of her pretty smiles.

"I release you from your promise." She stalked up to him and planting a finger firmly on his chest. Shoving, she shouted, "Go."

"You cannot release me from my word," he lied. In truth, according to their customs, she could. "I have given it. I'll see it through."

"Oh." she huffed, wanting to strike him but not so foolish as to try. "You are so... so... *argh*."

The high-pitched scream echoed over the pass. Rhiannon turned from him, storming down the path until she was out of sight. Sinking behind a boulder, she crossed her arms and stared at the beautiful sunset. It brought her no pleasure.

Ilar let her go. If he kept speaking to her, he'd probably only strangle her anyway to keep her quiet—or to keep from kissing her. Even now his body longed for her. It had been aching for her touch all day. So much so, that he'd refused to let her ride upon his back because he knew he could never stand the torture of it. And there was no way in heaven or hell he'd let her wrap her long legs around his friend, even if it was in travel.

"Accursed enchantment," he swore, as he went to gather firewood. But even as he said it, he knew the enchantment had nothing to do with his desire for her. It would have been there without it.

MALAK CAME BACK TO THE CAMPSITE WITH THREE large fish. They didn't look like any Rhiannon recognized, but as her stomach growled, she wasn't about to be picky. He glanced at her as he walked up the hillside, to where she sat beside a boulder, before looking higher up the path to where Ilar had started a fire in a rock clearing cut into the cliffs. He carried a knife in his hands and she hoped he didn't expect her to gut and clean them.

Malak's kilt-like attire wrapped his waist and hung to his knees. Like the other lycans, he was muscled. Seeing him did not give her the same reaction that Ilar's body did.

"It would be warmer by the firelight, my lady."

Rhiannon blinked, glancing over at Ilar. "I think it's colder by the firelight."

Ilar pretended not to hear her.

Malak looked over to where Ilar stared sullenly into the flames. The high rock face would protect them from the wind during the night. They made camp for the sake of Lady Rhiannon, who appeared worn from the day's travel. Neither lycan was tired. They drew strength from the night, able to travel at higher speeds while it was cool.

Malak was sympathetic, knowing how hard Ilar could seem to the fairer sex—especially a human who didn't have the ability to read him. Only if she were to become his lifemate would she gain the gift of his mind. Ilar was a man of duty and not always the clearest when it came to how he felt.

"Come, lady," Malak said. "These mountain passes grow cold during the dark hours and you never know what will lurk within the night shadows. It's much safer by the fire."

Rhiannon shot up to her feet in surprise, looking around the darkening countryside. Malak hid his grin as he began walking away. He and Ilar would sense anything that came near and there was nothing lurking in the shadows. But, let her have reason to seek Ilar's company. She looked like she desperately wanted to. After having spent the day hearing fragments of his friend's disconcerted thoughts, he'd bet Ilar would be more than willing to offer her protection—needed or not.

Rhiannon rushed behind Malak, coming close to his back as she tried to see out into the surrounding valley. She couldn't make out anything but was convinced some evil waited out in the darkness. Her skin prickled in warning, a sure sign that she should be worried. Malak stopped beneath the cliff path leading up the incline to Ilar. Rhiannon, preoccupied with the thought of demons, ran into his back, tripping over to the side. With his free hand, Malak grabbed her about the waist to keep her from falling.

Ilar came in time to see Rhiannon leaning over Malak's arm. Malak pushed her up and back, shielding her from Ilar's misunderstanding. With his mind, he tried to tell the Commander that nothing happened.

Ilar, angry and jealous, turned and stormed away from them.

Malak nodded his head for Rhiannon to climb before him. The incline wasn't steep, and she made it with little effort. Coming across the clearing, she saw Ilar's back was to her. Malak came up behind her, brushing past to go to the fire. Within moments, he set up a spit and was cooking their supper. No one said a word.

24

RHIANNON SIGHED IN EXHAUSTION. WITH A FULL stomach, she was glad they were not traveling through the night. Malak had found some herbs by the stream and she was pleased to discover he was an accomplished cook. When she said as much, Ilar just grunted. He ate in silence, throwing accusing glares at her and his friend.

Malak ignored Ilar's ill-humor, holding polite conversation with Rhiannon about Fenris. When the meal was finished, he stood, announcing, "I need to stretch my legs," before he strode from the campsite. Rhiannon noticed that there was a restlessness to Malak, a searching look that always appeared to be beyond what he was doing. He hopped from the cliff in a way she would never attempt.

Ilar grabbed a wine pouch and moved away from the fire.

Rhiannon watched as Malak took off in wolf form down the valley. Nervous now that she and Ilar were alone, she stood, drawn to him. She followed his gaze up to the silver moon. It was half full.

"The moon doesn't look like this back home," she said, almost sorrowful. She missed her family when she stopped to think about them.

Ilar knew the moment she joined him. Malak still tried to reason with him through the mind link, but he could not hear it, didn't want to hear it. Anger was easier than the pain he knew was to come the moment she walked through the portal to go home. He felt her like he'd never felt anything, needed her like a man needed air and food. Whatever Cupid had done, the troll had exacted a most agonizing revenge disproportionate to any slight.

"I remember," he finally answered. "Your moon is yellow and blue, sometimes red."

"Oh," she breathed, recalling how old he was, how much longer he'd probably live past her death. It was better for her to be going, if only for that reason. Even if he asked her to stay, she'd only grow old as he stayed as handsome as this moment. Her heart ached. The thought brought tears to her eyes. It's not like he'd made her any promises. She couldn't demand anything from him. "I suppose you would. Do you ever miss it? Being in my world?"

"I don't think on it," he said truthfully. Ilar imagined he would think on it a lot more after he sent her back there.

"May I have a drink?" Her voice was as soft as a whisper. She was very aware of where he stood next to her. She didn't see a single star, though she stared right at them.

Ilar glanced down at his hand before lifting it to her. Her eyes didn't meet his as she took it. She held it in silence, before pulling it to her lips.

"What manner of creatures live in these mountains?" she asked, seeing all the dark crevices as she wiped her mouth on her hand.

"Dragons," Ilar said without thought, "goblins, trolls, pixies, griffins, cy—"

"I understand," Rhiannon broke in, moving closer to him.

Ilar felt her near his arm. Glancing down in surprise at her touch, he saw her face was turned to the shadows.

Trembling at the very idea of such things—some of which she had never even heard of—Rhiannon handed the pouch back to him and he capped it off. Biting her lip, she let her hand slink up his arm before resting on his bicep. "Are they here now, do you think?"

Ilar let his arm drape naturally around her shoulder before he thought to stop it. He paused, seeing if she would shrug away. Rhiannon breathed in sharply, looking up at him, her eyes wide, expectant and inviting.

"They will not harm you," he said. "This land is different, but it's no more dangerous than your world."

As Rhiannon saw the glinting of gold in his eye, she knew he lied to comfort her. This land was much more dangerous than her world—at least for her. She didn't have magic, didn't understand any of it.

"For me, a human, this world is perilous." She trailed her hand up to rest over his heart, absently feeling the muscles of his chest. He was so strong and never had she felt so weak. "Even if I spent a hundred years here, I don't think I'd understand it."

Or you, she added silently, feeling sad.

"I would protect you," he stated, hesitating, wondering at her tone.

"I know," she said. He'd sworn to do so. "I'm sorry you have the burden of it."

Ilar wondered at her words but didn't dare ask her to explain. Did she mean the burden of his heart? The burden of his feelings for her? Were they that obvious?

"Did you..." she began, unable to look at him. She

felt the burning of tears behind her eyes and quickly blinked them back.

"What?" Ilar lifted his hand to her chin so that he could study her face in the silver moonlight.

"Did you do what you did with me because of the curse?" Her gaze cut into him with its insecurity.

Suddenly, Ilar forgot his anger at her blatant overtures to Malak. Her lips were trembling, softened by darkness. They parted. Her eyes dipped over his face, unwittingly inviting him to kiss her. She had so much passion when they came together, but here she was, standing before him, defenseless. It was as if she didn't know her appeal, her power over him. He was glad for it. If she knew the control she had, she could crush him.

"Being with you," he said, drawn to her lips, "was never a curse."

Rhiannon gasped at the admission. It wasn't love ballads or poetry, but it was the best she'd probably ever get from him and it was so much better. The strong arm tightened on her waist as she wound her hands up to meet his neck, pulling his face to deepen the tenderness of his kiss.

Ilar growled in the back of his throat, loving the taste of her, craving the feel of her skin against him. They might be at odds during the day, but their bodies could no longer stop their draw than they could change the pull of the moon on the tides.

Rhiannon moaned in protest when he pulled back to study her. Wrapping her arms around his neck, she lifted herself onto her toes. She pressed her kisses to his mouth and moaned into him, "No, Ilar, don't stop."

Rhiannon delved her hands over the strong ridge of his shoulders, pushing the draping tunic off the side so she could explore his chest. Caressing his jaw with her lips, she moved to taste his neck, bite and lick his earlobe.

Ilar groaned, a throaty sound of pleasure as his hands glided over her hips to squeeze her tender backside. She explored every nuance of his chest and back, unable to get enough of his touch.

"I wish we had a bed," she said shyly into his ear as he began devouring her neck, kissing her, sucking love brands beneath the edge of her gown as he further marked her flesh as his territory. She loved the feel of him against her, loved that he didn't want her merely because of her enchantment.

"Who needs a bed?" he answered.

Rhiannon shivered at the passionate admission. He lifted her from the ground so that her legs parted against his hips and her feet dangled behind him. He supported her weight with two hands firmly planted on her rounded backside and walked with her to the edge of the cliff bottom. When he set her back down it was within a sheltered crevice in the cliff face. The firelight haloed his head, glowing softly. The length of his hair tickled her breasts and shoulders. His power and strength excited her.

"You mean," she gasped, feeling him tugging the hidden ties on her shoulder to free her breasts, "out here?"

Her body hummed with pleasure at the very idea.

"Yes, here." He nodded.

Ilar's shifting eyes met with hers. He teased her breasts, budding the nipples, claiming them, branding them with his hot touch. He took her hand and lifted it so she could grab onto a rocky projection in the cliff side.

Keeping his gaze focused intensely on her entranced one, he tore the tunic from his waist and pulled up her skirts. His forehead pressed into hers, his nose lying along her nose as he watched her every reaction, took in her desire. Her ragged breath fanned over his parted lips —a stirring caress all its own.

Ilar brought his body to her, lifting her legs to his waist, holding her up, his strong fingers pressed into the tender cheeks of her butt. She dropped her hands to his shoulders, kneading into him, understanding how he meant to join them. Rhiannon tried to lean forward for his kiss, but his eyes held her back as he nipped playfully at her swollen lips.

Ilar entered her slowly, letting her feel each aching movement of his claiming as he pushed into her. She was ready for him. He fitted and stretched her around his arousal. This time there would be no mistaking that she was marked as his. His brand would be all over her. His scent would be her scent. Rhiannon's mouth opened, her head drew back in ecstasy, her eyes drifted closed.

"No, Rhian," he demanded. "Look at me."

Surprised by the sternness of the command, she obeyed. Her mouth widened in a silent scream of pleasure as he pushed fully into her moist depths. He held himself there, deep, strong, filling.

"Ilar," she said, weak and needy. He still didn't move. Rhiannon squirmed against him. The rock at her back made it impossible to thrust herself against his distended flesh. She was trapped, at the mercy of his will.

"You are my lover, no one else's," Ilar stated possessively.

Rhiannon nodded in feverish agreement. She pushed her lips to his. He refused her. Why was he stopping? She didn't want any other lovers. She wanted him, needed him. She tried to force him to move, wiggling her hips against him.

He reached to press his finger along the artery at her

neck, fitting his thumb to the groove, as he found the soft divot at the base of her throat. He heard her racing heart beneath her breasts. Her chest rose and fell with heavy breath. He splayed his fingers over her jaw as if he could drive the admission out of her.

"Yes, Ilar," she gasped at last, giving herself over to him. His eyes pierced her soul, intent and demanding. "I belong to you, no one else."

A bestial growl left his throat as he gave her body what it craved. His lips crushed into hers as his hips thrust, moving deep and gentle inside her. Rhiannon's nails bit into his flesh, digging in mindless ecstasy. Her legs stretched and strained as she held on. When her clawing drew the slightest bit of blood, he groaned in delight that her passion matched his. His body healed itself instantly, unharmed by her rough, eager hold.

"Oh, Ilar... *ah*," she whimpered at the way he made her feel. She never wanted this moment to end. She bit into his lip with her teeth and stretched her tongue into his mouth.

"Rhian," he cried out, answering her call. Neither one noticed the dark night, the silver moon, nor the splendor of the crag Rhiannon was pressed against. All they saw and felt was each other.

"Ah, Ilar, that, I," she managed incoherently, unable to get her thoughts across as she tensed. His pace kept steady, working her to her climax. His body slid in her with ease, rocking against her hips. Suddenly, she screamed. Her hips bucked against him as her back arched into the hard stone. The stars sprinkled above her, blurring like trails of light through her half-closed lids.

Ilar's passionate cry joined hers as he felt her body convulse against him. He didn't stop, pumping faster as he sought his release. Finally, Ilar tensed, spilling himself into her, letting her have every last inch of his soul. Dropping forward, he bit lightly at her neck as the tremors slowly left them. He licked the thin bead of blood that followed.

She was incapable of getting what she was feeling past her lips. Never in her life did she imagine she could feel so much in one instant.

Ilar pulled himself from within her, letting her legs fall to the ground. Not backing away, he trapped her to the side of the cliff, beneath the protective fold of his body. Rhiannon let her hands fall lightly to his neck, rubbing along his jaw as he gently kissed her.

"*Mm,*" she lazily moaned against him. Without warning, her eyes popped open, and she pushed him back.

Ilar blinked in surprise. Rhiannon tried frantically to right her dress, a bright blush staining her cheeks with pink.

"What?" he asked, his senses alert. He detected no danger.

"What if Malak comes back?" she asked, frantic. It mortified her to think the man might have heard her screaming or that he might find them wantonly pressed to the stone.

Ilar frowned. He grabbed her jaw in his hand, forcefully moving her face to meet his. His eyes burned in possession. His scent was all over her. She was his. "You are my lover, not his."

Rhiannon balked, as she tried to slap him away. His grip kept her from lacing the ties on her shoulder so she could cover herself.

"Ilar, please," she begged, trying to pull away. "Stop."

To her surprise, he roared in anger. His lips were not soft and gentle when they moved to possess her mouth. She gasped, thrilled by his passion, but frightened by its intent. He forced his tongue into her mouth until she couldn't breathe anything but his breath.

Tears came fearfully to her eyes. Moaning in fear, she hit at him, trying to get him to back away. Ilar let her go, his chest heaving.

"Ilar, please," she pleaded, desperate, terrified and aroused by this side of him. "He'll see us."

"You dare to speak to me of him?" he demanded.

"What?" she asked, trying to burrow into the unforgiving stone. "What are you talking about? I only meant—"

"I know what you meant," he thundered. Taking his hand to her throat, he didn't squeeze. No matter how angry he was, he could never really hurt her. "Get this straight, Rhiannon. You are mine until I let you go."

Rhiannon trembled. She would have been pleased by the claim, had he not screamed it at her. His eyes were wild, possessed. She trembled. It had to be the enchantment. It wasn't gone. That's why he acted like this. That's why he came to her again. He was under a spell. He didn't really want her. It was only the spell.

Rhiannon cried, unable to stop the flow of tears that poured over her flushed cheeks. It was a wretched heartbreak, clouding over the passion in her limbs.

Ilar drew back at the sudden burst of grief. His eyes took her in as she crumbled to her hands and knees on the stone, weeping.

"Rhiannon," he began, automatically reaching to comfort her.

"Don't touch me," she said. "Don't you dare touch me."

Ilar's mouth snapped shut, pressing into a hard line. Her eyes glared out at him, bitter and hard. His chest caved in on itself until he was sure his heart would never beat again. Stiffly, he nodded, turning to go back to the campfire.

Rhiannon didn't move. Huddled in the dark corner, she righted her dress the best she could. Her legs wouldn't support her. Ilar didn't come for her again and it was there she fell into a troubled sleep.

Malak spent the night alone in a comfortable cave in lycan form, not wanting to bother the two lovers. He heard their cries of passion as he ran the mountain trails. His heart had been gladdened that they finally got over their stubbornness. But as he came back to the campsite early with the dawn to see Ilar staring moodily at the flames and Rhiannon missing, he wasn't so sure.

"Where is Lady Rhiannon?" Malak asked Ilar carefully. For a moment, he froze. Ilar's face looked as if he could have committed murder.

Jerking his thumb up the cliff, Ilar pointed to where she still slept behind the jutting of rocks.

Malak frowned, relieved when he detected the slight sound of her breathing. As he came around the corner, he found her huddled in the rock face. Her body trembled with cold as she slept and she used her own hair as a blanket. Leaving her where she was, Malak came around to glare at his friend. "What did you do to her?"

Ilar merely grunted.

'By all that is sacred, Ilar, look at her.' Malak directed so as not to scare Rhiannon. *'She's freezing.'*

"You look at her," Ilar grumbled aloud. "I'm done with her."

'You marked her as yours, Ilar. She's yours to deal with,' Malak raged. He strode down the path and began slowly stripping out of his clothes.

"Where are you going?" Ilar asked, standing.

"I go to hunt down Cupid," Malak answered with an angry scowl. "He has to be somewhere within these caves. His pungent scent shouldn't be too hard to hunt down. I'll leave my satchel with you for Rhiannon. Once I have him tracked, I'll send word. Until then, you put things right with her. I want no more in the middle of you two."

Malak leapt down onto the lower path. Ilar didn't watch as Malak's body blurred into a vision of raven black fur.

"Where's Malak going?" Rhiannon asked, yawning. Malak's lycan form ran into the distance, his tunic clutched in his mouth. She'd barely heard them talking, not knowing what they said in their bestial tongue. She flinched as she stretched her tense muscles.

"Sorry to see him go?" Ilar asked bitterly. He hadn't slept.

Rhiannon flinched again, this time at his sharp tone. Ilar stood, kicking dirt onto the remnants of the dying fire.

"Just sorry my only decent company is gone," Rhiannon grumbled. When Ilar's hard gaze flew to look at her, she frowned.

She watched in silence as Ilar packed up the campsite. When he came to her, she tensed, her eyes hungrily devouring his face for a tender sentiment of any kind. He thrust Malak's satchel at her and said, "Here. Eat while we travel."

Rhiannon took the satchel from him and hefted it over her shoulder. It was heavy and weighted her steps, but she didn't complain. Ilar didn't wait for her as he leapt off the rise and began a swift pace.

Rhiannon struggled to follow him, climbing down with much less grace than he. Then, running, she rushed to catch up to his fast stride. Ilar merely glanced at her, not saying a word as he jogged.

THE STITCH IN HER SIDE WAS KILLING HER. IT HAD started as a minor annoyance about an hour before but soon grew to a sharp pain that strained her already sore body to the point of exhaustion. Ilar's jog soon turned into a run down the side of the mountains. He didn't seem to notice the weight of his satchel and his endurance was tireless.

After three hours of traveling and stumbling without a break or food, Rhiannon's body was pushed to the limit. The satchel pulled her down, pressing into her shoulder, shooting pains up her neck. Looking ahead, she came to a stop. Ilar was before her, running ever forward.

Let him go, she thought bitterly, swaying on her feet, beyond caring. Her body was drenched in sweat. Her long locks were plastered to her head. She'd wished more than once she could stop to bind them from her face. The clip she'd used the day before was long lost back at the campsite, most likely when she and Ilar made love.

Rhiannon frowned. Could it be called making love when a spell forced him to her? Never had she felt more repulsive. It was like paying a man to be with her, or blackmailing or bribing him.

Rhiannon let the weight of the satchel take her down as she fainted, too tired to fight. She felt herself falling but didn't care. The blackness was inviting and her mind grabbed hold of it, numbing her to everything else.

Ilar felt the distance spanning between them and stopped to turn around. Rhiannon stood, weaving gingerly in the breeze. She said she could run, and he hadn't thought to question her claim. She hadn't once asked him to slow or stop. In fact, she'd said nothing to him.

Frowning, he took a step toward her. The long strands of her hair blew, stretching like silken waves over the side of the mountain base. The satchel's weight pulled her to the side, following the trail of her hair. Ilar panicked as her body swayed again. He ran as fast as his legs would carry him, swiftly darting to her side.

Ilar would never forget how his heart stopped as she fell limply over the edge of the cliff. Leaping into the air, he soared forward, blindly diving after her. He caught her in his arms, blocking her body as they slid and bounced down the rocky incline.

The rocks tore up his back as he held her. They slowly skidded to a stop, rolling over each other as they came to the end. Rhiannon flew out of his arms and cried out.

Ilar grunted, crawling to her, ignoring his pain. The wounds on his back would heal themselves. Her hands were tossed above her head, lying over her golden curls. His heart stopped beating to look at her. She was so beautiful to him.

Rhiannon's ankle throbbed were it had struck something. She stared at the purple sky, seeing the haze of violet clouds overhead. The wind had been knocked out of her and she gasped for each breath. Suddenly, a shadow cast across her face and Ilar's hair cocooned her to block out the bright light. The dark handsomeness of him was so much better a view than the sky had been. She could spend the rest of her life looking at him.

"I needed a small rest." It felt too good to hold still, so she didn't move. Her world spun with the effect of their fall.

"Foolish woman," he said, relieved she kept her wits. Looking up at the cliff, he saw it hadn't been as steep as he first feared.

"You saved my life," she said in awe, staring at his

handsome, devilish eyes. She instantly heated toward him at the look on his proud features.

Ilar again glanced up the incline. Giving her a smile that made her heart stop, he said, "Hardly."

Rhiannon grabbed his face with a sudden burst of energy, taking his mouth to hers in a desperate kiss that said everything she dared not. Her mouth pressed into his firm lips, remembering the feel of them all too well. She needed him, wanted him, craved him. He was so stubborn, so frustrating and proud. He made her want to scream and tear every gorgeous inch of his hair out. But when his eyes looked at her so openly, she couldn't stop herself. She had to kiss him. When she grew too weak to hold her body up, she fell away, panting, staring at him.

"What was that?" he asked, licking his lips still stinging with her taste.

"I don't know," she said, dreamily, breathless. "I felt like doing it."

"Do it again," he urged, tilting his head down to hers, not giving her a choice. His mouth moved against her, passionate, demanding, searching.

Rhiannon chuckled, grabbing his face to keep him near her, pulling at his back when she would feel more of his body pressed along hers. The thick set of his erection burned into her stomach, teasing her through their clothes. She forgot everything but the sensation of him against her.

Sensing movement in the light shining through her closed lids, she gasped, pushing frantically at Ilar's chest. A scream bubbled in her throat.

"Careless human watch where you're falling," a small green piskie screeched. He had big eyes that looked cute and innocent, but the expression on his face said otherwise. Suddenly, Rhiannon realized that she must have struck the poor being with her foot when she fell. The creature wielded a small knife as if it would stab her.

Ilar turned, growling at the little pest, snapping his jaw as if he would bite it. The creature ran off, taking great leaps over the grass to make good his escape. When he turned back to resume his kisses, Rhiannon had already withdrawn. The spell between them was broken. Her stormy eyes were fixed overhead, her body stiff, and Ilar heard the roar of a far-off dragon.

"Just get me home, Ilar," she whimpered in fright. She'd been through too much—seen too much. Now tiny green beings wanted her dead and there was fire spouting across the sky from a giant winged beast. She cringed away from the flying dragon.

Ilar thought she moved from him, as she recoiled into the ground. A pain ripped through his chest.

"Please, Ilar, I want to go home," she said.

Frowning, Ilar rolled off her body. His limbs stung in protest. His arousal ached to be inside her, always inside her. It didn't matter how often he tasted the pleasure of her, he wanted her again, each time worse than before.

Holding his hand to her, he watched as she hesitated, her eyes turned to the purple sky. Slowly, her palm fitted into his and he jerked her up. Rhiannon winced in pain, her ankle folding underneath her as she tripped.

Ilar instantly lifted her into his arms. Striding over the field, he leapt back up the incline with her gripped tightly to his chest. Rhiannon gasped and burrowed deeper into his embrace. Bringing her to a shady knoll of grass, hidden from the direct rays of the sun, he set her down. Her arms didn't wish to leave his neck and stubbornly held their place when he would pull back.

"Rhian," he said, his tone almost sultry. Catching himself, as he drew forward to kiss her, he demanded, "Where does it hurt?"

Rhiannon could think of a few places. Instead, she said, "My ankle."

"Here, let me see it," he ordered. Rhiannon released his neck to lie back on the grass. Ilar pulled the edge of her gown up slowly. After quickly assessing it, he discovered it was only bruised. "It isn't broken."

"It feels like it," she complained, a pout on her features. She'd been studying him as he tenderly took care of her. His gentle hands did something to her leg, making the nerves jump in wanton excitement.

Without warning, Ilar stood, his head tilting to the side.

"What is it?" Rhiannon asked, pushing up. "Is the dragon coming back?"

"No," Ilar said, distracted. He held up his hand for silence. "Malak has found Cupid's cave. He wants us to wait here until he gets back. Then we will go confront the little troll."

Rhiannon stiffened. So soon? As much as she hated being cursed, she hated the idea of not being cursed even more. Would all the affection Ilar showered on her be taken back? Would he recoil from her in repulsion? Her whole body shook. "When?"

"Tomorrow morn. It's just as well. You need to rest your ankle." Ilar glanced around. "This place will suit us fine. You stay here. I'll gather wood and try to catch food."

She searched the heavens for signs of the dragon.

He reached into his satchel and pulled out a knife. He handed it to her. "Use it if you have a need."

Rhiannon nodded, gripping the blade as she pushed against the rock to hide from the sky beneath an overhang. Within a full breath, Ilar was gone, over the side of the rock face and into the valley below.

ILAR CAME BACK AN HOUR LATER AND SET UP A cooking fire. It was evening and Rhiannon was more than happy to see him. He eyed her warily, noticing she still clutched the knife. Without comment, he worked and soon turned what looked like rabbits on a spit.

Rhiannon offered to help, but he told her to relax. She was content to watch. It wasn't like she could cook anyway. Gingerly, she hobbled over to him when he'd finished, leaving the rabbits to roast. She looked down at the top of his dark head as she stood by his side. Ilar glanced up in surprise to feel her so near and stood to tower over her. The disarming look in his eyes penetrated her.

When he would turn away, Rhiannon placed a hand on his arm to stop him. She'd been given a lot of time to think about it and if she only had this one last night of enchantment, she intended to use it to full advantage. "Is there a place I can bathe? I feel like I'm covered in dust and sweat."

Ilar blinked at the question, but lifting his head in the air, he closed his eyes and inhaled. When he again looked at her, he said, "Up there."

Rhiannon looked up the steep mountainside, doubting she could climb with her sore ankle.

Ilar, sensing her dilemma, asked, "Would you like me to help you up?"

Rhiannon nodded, brimming with excitement as he swung her into his arms. She clung to his neck. Her jaw rested on his shoulder as she hugged herself to him. He instantly stiffened. She ran her hands over his upper back, sending shivers over his flesh as she dipped her fingernails slightly beneath the folds of his draping blue tunic.

Ilar carried her up the steep incline. Then reaching the top, he smiled to see the water just where he detected it. Setting Rhiannon on the ground, he heard her gasp of pleasure. They were before a little pond surrounded with the sprinkling of flower-covered earth. The clear waters reflected the brilliance of the purple sky. It looked as if they were in the heavens, though higher mountains still rose up on each side.

Ilar looked her over, his body tight from holding her so close. He nodded once and turned to leave.

"Wait," she called to him, reaching her hand out.

A brow arched, slashing over his penetrating gaze. He shifted his weight to look at her. His long hair covered his face partially from view.

"Would you stay?" she asked, trembling as she made the request.

"You have nothing to fear from these waters," he soothed. In truth, he didn't wish to put himself through the torture of watching her bathe. "You have no need of my protection. And if you do, you only have to call and I'll be here."

Rhiannon took a deep breath. Her eyes met his. "I didn't mean for you to stay as my protector."

Ilar froze. His whole body filled with molten desire.

"I meant for you to stay as my lover." Though the words were shy, she held her ground, watching him.

A slow, amazed smile found his lips. He couldn't speak. Rhiannon pulled at the laces of her gown, freeing herself from the dirty material. It slithered off her body, heaping at her feet.

Ilar's breath caught. His heart nearly stopped. She stood before him, naked and proud, outlined by the sunlight.

Her breasts rose and fell with her deepened breathing, so perfect in shape. He itched to mold them into his palms, to bud the tips to his sucking lips. She parted her legs, drawing attention to her hair-covered mound. Already, the scent of her was carried to him on the breeze until he wanted nothing more than to bury his face and drink from her most intimate of openings.

Rhiannon forced herself not to move as he looked her over. A blush heated her cheeks. The fire in his gaze stoked her desires. Slowly, she took a step back, edging to the pond.

Ilar's attention stayed with her. He saw her vulnerable eyes, amazing him still with their almost innocent quality. He grabbed the brooch from his shoulder. Without thought, he tugged the clothing from his body until he was as naked as she.

It was Rhiannon's turn to look, and she did, taking in her fill of him until every dip and flex was well ingrained in her mind. The hair sprinkling his thighs rose around his erection. She'd seen him before, but never had she been so bold as to take in every detail of his arousal. The globes beneath his shaft looked larger, heavier than she remembered.

She backed away, her feet hitting upon cooler water. A shiver worked its way up her spine. "Would you swim with me, Ilar?"

Ilar forgot all about the cooking rabbits over the fire

as he stepped into the pond after her. Rhiannon continued back, keeping her gaze steadily on him as the water rose around her hips. The curly length of her hair floated around her on the glass surface. The reflection of clouds rippled as she moved. Ilar was sure he'd never seen anything so stunning in all his life.

Lowering herself into the pond, Rhiannon swam back. She dipped her face beneath the water, resurfacing to stroke backward as she watched him dive in to join her. He glided beneath the waves and with one stroke he reached her. He slithered his hands over her flesh beneath the water, finding her hips as he moved to stand.

"Would you make love to me, Ilar?" she asked, breathless with anticipation. She knew if he denied her, she'd surely die.

He pushed the long length of his hair from his dark features. His eyes were a molten gold as he looked at her. He lifted her and buried his face in her breasts as he licked and teased the nipples into erect points. Her legs wrapped his waist, slipping over his butt and hips.

Rhiannon's head arched back on her shoulders and she cried out in pleasure. He drank from her flesh, licking her with his tongue as he sent shockwaves all over her body. She practically melted around him.

She delved her fingers into his hair, pulling the length back from his face so she could see his masculine beauty. His eyes rose to meet hers, heavy-lidded with pleasure. Her head dipped, wanting more than anything to kiss him. She moaned into his mouth, drawing heat from his skin. His hands felt like they were everywhere at once. His thick erection pressed near her backside as he lowered her against his solid frame. Her thighs pressed into his stomach, the hard ridge of his muscles rubbing against her.

"Is this what you want?" he asked. His kiss deepened, probing and claiming every corner of her mouth, stealing inside her to grab at her soul.

Rhiannon shivered, knowing this man branded her in more ways than one. Her legs worked against him, urging his hips closer as she tightened her hold.

"Yes, Ilar," she said, urging him on. Her toes curled, her back flexed, frenzied by the feel of him. She wiggled in frustration. She tried to pull up, wanting to force herself down onto his arousal.

Ilar held her firm, and she was no match for his strength. He kept her body from claiming him, continuing to kiss her throat, her collarbone and finally the valley of her breasts.

"Ilar, please," she begged, growing fevered as she rubbed herself on his stomach, searching for release. She pulled insistently at his shoulders and arms, loving the slick texture of his skin.

"Tell me you want me inside you," he demanded.

"Yes, I want you inside me." Her hips pushed faster in her frustration. The water splashed them, rippling at her movements.

"Tell me I'm the only man you'll ever want."

Rhiannon shivered, looking into his eyes. She knew it was the enchantment making him speak, but she couldn't stop herself from answering, "You're the only man I've ever wanted inside me, Ilar. The only man I'll ever want."

His heart leapt with hope at the soft admission. Instantly, he slid into her heated folds, fitting himself firmly to her core.

"Ah," she whimpered, surprised that each time they came together he could fill her so completely. His length stretched her. Her mouth opened with wide pants along his lips. She darted her tongue to lick playfully at him. He growled, sucking her tongue into his mouth as he moved within her. Her hair clung to her shoulders.

The surface of the water undulated around them. Rhiannon held his shoulders, driving herself onto him with desperation and fear. She never wanted these feelings to end. She wanted to pull him with her and hide away forever in the mountains, keeping him enchanted by her spell. Tears came to her eyes. He firmly grasped her backside, digging at her flesh, as he rocked inside her.

Heat shot through her limbs, crashing over her like the rippling water, moving along her trembling skin as she climaxed. Rhiannon cried out. She pushed down, imbedding him deep.

Ilar howled as he met his release. His legs weakened and they dipped beneath the surface, kissing before they resurfaced. Rhiannon wrapped her arms around him, holding him close, glad that the water washed away her tears before he could see them.

Ilar's weight shifted. Thinking he meant to pull away, she begged, "No. Not yet. Don't go yet."

Ilar gently kissed her. His body was sated from her lovemaking, but as she continued to touch him, running her hands over his hair and shoulders like she needed to feel every inch of him, he felt himself stirring once more against her stomach.

Rhiannon's eyes widened, growing excited at the intimate press of him. Her gaze dipped shyly to his mouth, pressing wet kisses along his firm lips to his neck, only to nibble at his ear. He hugged her closer until not even the water could slip between their bodies.

She shivered at the strength of his embrace. "Will you make love to me again?"

Ilar growled, turning to devour her neck and shoulder. Sweeping her up into his arms, he carried her over to the shore. Rhiannon shivered as he tenderly laid her on the grassy banks, surrounded by flowers. The purple, magenta, and orange sunset was all around them. The water lapped gently at the pond's shore.

Rhiannon looked up at him, offering her whole body. Anything he wanted, she would give him. It was too late for her. The lycan warrior forever enthralled her. Without him she would be hopeless and lost. She had a feeling that the rest of her life would be spent in a tower, remembering this moment.

Ilar's eyes dipped leisurely over her flesh, stroking his hands in short passes over her neck, her chest, her aching breasts. His mouth soon followed to trail over her flesh. He took his time savoring her feel, her taste. Only after he'd touched and kissed every inch of her, did he rise above her.

Ilar looked deeply into her eyes as he lifted on his hands. He tensed as he stroked within the slick fires he'd started. Almost desperately, Rhiannon clung to his arms, rocking into him, pushing him deeper, urging him harder, faster. The beast took over, claiming her, untamed and vigorous. Rhiannon cried out, loving this animalistic side to him. As the last of their violent tremors subsided, they both instinctively knew that this could very well be their last night together.

ILAR MADE LOVE TO RHIANNON SO MANY TIMES THAT her limbs were sore and twisted from his endless stamina and positions. During the middle of their love play, Ilar carried her down to the campfire. The rabbits were burnt, but they didn't care. Instead, they drank wine—Rhiannon from the pouch, Ilar from her breasts and neck. Only when her body refused to move more than the effort it took to keep breathing, did Ilar gather her naked body into his arms and wrap them in the large square piece of his draping tunic. It was there they slept.

The next morning, Rhiannon awoke to a feathery kiss along her temple. Groaning, she covered her yawn and peeked up into Ilar's solid brown eyes. Even with his hair disheveled, he was devilishly handsome to behold.

The soft golden rays of morning cast over his skin. Without thought, she smiled, reaching to touch him.

Suddenly, his head jerked away, looking into the distance. Rhiannon stiffened as she heard a deep, masculine chuckle behind her head. Horrified at being caught, she burrowed her naked body into Ilar's, trying to hide.

Ilar wrapped a protective arm around her, wondering at her sudden shyness, before glancing up to where Malak stood. When Malak spoke, Rhiannon couldn't understand his words and what she imagined him to say was much worse than what he said.

"Glad to see you put things right," Malak said, still laughing heartily. He sauntered into the campsite, not thinking anything of the couple lying together. It was only natural for lovers to do so. Besides, being a race that stripped down to the nude at a moment's notice no matter where they were, being naked was no big affair and deserved no more notice than walking around in clothes.

Malak eyed the two crispy rabbits and frowned, wrinkling his nose in disgust of the waste.

Ilar grinned sheepishly. Rhiannon said something against his chest that neither lycan could understand. When Ilar tried to pull her face back to study her, she nestled deeper beneath the tunic in an effort to hide herself.

Ilar's expression fell. He glanced at Malak.

Malak shrugged, confused, as he looked over the spray of golden curls coming from beneath the draping tunic, spilling forth from Ilar's chest.

With a tilt of his jaw, Ilar beckoned his friend to move away from the campsite.

"Might as well," Malak grumbled, as he turned to go. "It doesn't look as if you'll be cooking to break our fast."

Rhiannon didn't hear him go. All she heard was the growling language of the lycans. She shivered, huddling closer.

Ilar put a hand on her shoulder and gently tried to pry her away. Rhiannon shook her head furiously and reached her arms around his waist to hold on for dear life.

"Are you so upset to be claimed by me?" Ilar asked, hurt.

At the whisper next to her temple, Rhiannon relaxed her hold but didn't free herself from his chest. Oh, but the sound of his voice could easily melt her. She pulled back enough to whisper, "Is he gone?"

"Yes, it's just us," Ilar said. She instantly relaxed. Ilar studied her flushed features. If he had to guess, he would say she was thoroughly embarrassed.

Ilar found her naked hip and rubbed it in slow, absent circles. Rhiannon, mistaking his innocent affection as another invitation at love play, pushed his hand from her hip. Looking over her shoulder, she tried to sit up.

"No, Ilar, we cannot," she said, her eyes darting around.

"You can't have two lovers, Rhian," Ilar stated with a scowl. "It doesn't work like that for the lycan. If you are my lover, you can't go to Malak. If you wanted him, you shouldn't have let me claim you as mine. You should have stated it was only a body affair."

Rhiannon shivered at his low, sultry words, even if they were clipped with angry. Then, comprehending what he said about Malak, she frowned. "Malak? You think I wish for Malak to be my...?"

She couldn't finish the sentence. It was too hilarious to comprehend. Rhiannon giggled. Ilar shot up, pulling away from her. Rhiannon reached for him, tugging on his arm to bring him back.

"Ilar, wait," she said.

"What?" he demanded. "I'll not be laughed at."

"I'm not laughing at you," she explained, almost bashful as he made her say the words. "It's the idea that you think... that I could be... well, you know, like this with *him*."

With anyone else but you, she added silently. Her cheeks only grew pinker.

His eyes narrowed. His senses picked up her heartbeat, ready to detect her lie. "Why do you hide as if you are ashamed?"

Her eyes round in shock, she said, "Well, I was..."

Rhiannon swallowed nervously, pulling the draping tunic to her exposed chest, much to Ilar's disappointment. Her wild tangle of curls spiraled from her head, untamed because they'd dried while he made love to her.

Rhiannon hugged the garment to her, baring more of him. As she saw the contours of his body, she grew warm with the all too familiar pull of his appeal. Forcing her gaze away, she tried to finish, "Well, we weren't... *suitable* to receive guests."

As if a ton of rocks slid down and landed on his head, Ilar finally understood. She wasn't ashamed because she wanted Malak. She was merely modest at being caught in such *unsuitable* positions. Ilar growled, pulling her into his arms and rolling her on top of him. She winced as her ankle jarred, but the rest had done it good and she didn't complain as he held her cheek to his chest.

Stroking the soft blonde curls from her face, he said, "You don't need to be ashamed of being caught in my arms. It's perfectly acceptable to be with your lover. It isn't a secret what lovers do, Rhian."

"My people are not so open." Being pressed intimately above him, Rhiannon began getting some unsuitable ideas of her own. Wiggling, as her legs fell over his sides to straddle his waist, she asked, "Can you use your mind-thing to keep Malak away for a while longer?"

Ilar grinned but nodded. He was entranced by her beauty, by the feel of her body.

Rhiannon purred as she began exploring the beastly man beneath her. She rose up, letting her body soak in the warming sunlight of the morning. A breeze whipped her hair about her shoulders.

Rhiannon kissed him all over, exploring each curve of him with her fingers. Then when she trailed her kisses down his stomach, Ilar tensed, waiting, grunting with anticipation, howling in pleasure as her lips moved past his navel.

Her hair tickled his rigid flesh. She licked a muscular, perfect hip. Running her cheek over the sleek fire of his arousal, she kissed him there too, along the unyielding shaft. When he didn't object, she did it again, growing bolder with each pass of her lips.

"Ah, woman," he said, his hands tangling into her curls. "You will undoubtedly be the death of me."

Rhiannon didn't understand his words as they rolled out in his bestial language. Pulling back, she asked, "Did you tell me to stop?"

Ilar reached up, pulling her firmly on top of his lap so she sat astride him. "I'd never tell you to stop, my lady."

He kissed her, deep and hard. Rhiannon whimpered, stunned to breathlessness as her body sung to fiery life.

"I'll never get enough of you. I like it when your lips are on me. I like the feel of your soft mouth against my body. I like the feel of your skin to mine." Between each declaration, he seared her lips with his wet, hungry kisses.

"You're under a spell," she said, sadly.

Instead of answering with words, which Ilar wasn't sure would be received as the truth, he answered her with his body. Lifting her, he lowered her onto him.

Rhiannon gasped, melting against him as he rocked her against his hips. Her forehead pressed down to his as she rode him, gaining momentum until their bodies exploded. Their heavy breaths mingled together as their hearts managed to slow by degrees.

"Can I come up yet?" came an irritated growl from below. "I have food and I care not what you are doing."

Rhiannon's cheeks flamed, but her neglected stomach grumbled loudly in response. Ilar chuckled at her innocent expression of dismay. It was out of place considering they were in such a wanton position.

Rhiannon wiggled off his lap. Searching around for clothing, she gulped, looking up by the pond where her dirty gown still lay.

"Malak," Ilar yelled.

"Aye?" came the answering call. Ilar could detect humor in his friend's gruff voice.

"Toss me half your tunic," Ilar said.

"No, it's my best one."

Ilar growled. Suddenly, they heard a rip and half of Malak's tunic came flying over the edge of the cliff.

Catching it, Ilar wrapped it around his waist. It left his chest bare. Then, grabbing his draping blue tunic, he made quick work of fashioning a gown for Rhiannon, clasping it with his brooch right above her breast. His eyes shone wickedly as his hand brushed over her nipple, purposefully making her tremble. When she was covered, he called Malak.

Malak jumped up on the cliff, eyeing Rhiannon and Ilar with a grin of amusement. Without saying a word, he tossed the charred rabbits aside and replaced them with fish.

RHIANNON'S NEW GOWN SMELLED OF ILAR, MAKING it hard to concentrate. To her relief, she found her ankle didn't hurt nearly as badly as she'd thought it would, and they again began the journey to Cupid's cave. The flowers along the pathway became tattered and torn as if they'd been kicked repeatedly. With each step, her heart fell deeper and deeper into the knotted pit of her stomach.

The troll's cave home was just that—a cave. There was no door, no welcoming indication that anything lived in the little hole carved inside the mountain. Judging by the smell wafting out of the darkness, Rhiannon wasn't so sure Cupid was still alive.

Sidling up to Malak, she wrinkled her nose and asked, "Are you sure you didn't kill him already?"

Ilar and Malak glanced down at the top of her head. Seeing her gag in disgust, they hid their smirks.

Ilar nodded his head at Malak and then to the cave, indicating for him to go and get the little troll. Malak shook his head furiously, saying through the mind link, *'I tracked him, you retrieve him.'*

Rhiannon frowned, seeing them glare at each other and motion frantically to the cave opening. Rolling her eyes, she stepped forward, peeking inside.

"Oh, Cupid," she called sweetly into the rotten depths. "I have brought you my lycan enthralls to play with. Come out and let's have some fun with them. I think your magic fades and I would have the whole Lycan Guard at my command barking like a chorus of singing dogs."

Ilar and Malak shared grimacing looks.

It didn't take long for a head to peek out the front of the cave entrance. Cupid's beady black eyes blinked as he looked first at Rhiannon and then at the two lycans behind her. When Ilar and Malak didn't move, a wide grin spread over his thick lips and he scratched thoughtfully at the inside of his overlarge nose.

"I need more magic, Cupid, please," Rhiannon said. He was still out of reach and she didn't relish the idea of diving in after him.

Cupid eyed her suspiciously.

"Here, I'll prove they're under my spell. Watch." Rhiannon turned to the men, a smirk lining her very mischievous features, as she said, "Ilar, hop on one foot."

Malak hid his amusement, but Ilar heard his friend's laughter in his head. Dutifully, he obeyed. Rhiannon's eyes lit slightly as his clothing bounced up, revealing his thighs. She glanced at Cupid, expectant. He wasn't convinced.

"Malak," Rhiannon called harmoniously, her voice almost a pout. "Transform to your lycan form and back for me."

Malak grunted but did as he was told, adjusting his clothes when he was finished. Rhiannon didn't turn, watching Cupid as he crept closer.

"Have them do something not so simple," Cupid commanded, his eyes lighting with pleasure.

"Ilar, Malak," Rhiannon said, leaning over slightly so Cupid couldn't see them behind her back. "Kiss."

She could feel their outrage.

Ilar and Malak glanced at each other, grimacing. They didn't move. They much rather dive into the smelly hole and fish out the troll. Cupid, not wanting to miss such a devious sight, darted forward. Rhiannon grabbed the putrid troll and held on. He knocked her over while trying to get free.

"Ilar," Rhiannon screamed, "help me."

Malak grabbed Cupid from her arms, lifting the troll.

Ilar stood above her, his hands placed firmly on his hips. Then, reaching down, he helped her up, grumbling, "Kiss?"

"If you insist," she murmured impishly in return, placing a quick kiss on Ilar's lips. His eyes softened by a small degree. Malak cleared his throat, reminding them of what they were doing.

"What do you wish to do with him, my lady?" Malak asked, holding the troll up by the back of his dirty trousers.

"I say we bathe him and cover him in flowers," Rhiannon stated. "Unless he tells me why he did this to me."

Cupid screamed in agony at the very idea. "Ugly mortal. Evil, wicked, ugly mortal."

Rhiannon stepped forward in warning. She reached down to pick a lovely pink flower. She wielded it at him like a blade. Cupid squirmed. "Don't make me put this in your nose."

"It's your fault, human," Cupid spat. "I inadvertently help out one couple and you all dub me a cherub. Now the whole mortal realm thinks I'm a chubby little babe who shoots arrows of love. And you, Lord Ilar, made the whole court believe that I have no power. Well, now I think you know the true extent of my magic. Neither world will ever doubt me again."

"Tell me why the spell isn't broken, Cupid," Rhiannon demanded. "Or so help, me I'll kiss that horrid little mouth of yours."

She moved her lips as if to pucker. Ilar couldn't resist, he chuckled.

Cupid squirmed, screaming in agony and pain at the very idea. "The only way to end it is for Lord Ilar to mate with you."

"I did mate with her," Ilar said. "The enchantment isn't gone."

Despite herself, Rhiannon felt her cheeks flame at the bold announcement. Did none of them have an ounce of modesty?

"Ah," Cupid said, "not as a lover, but as a lifemate. Only when she's lifemated will the enchantment end."

Rhiannon asked in surprise, "We'd have to wed?"

"Not just human wed," Cupid said, kicking in the air. "Lifemates bound forever. A marriage you can escape. This you cannot."

Her rounded gaze found Ilar. She couldn't breathe. She couldn't bind herself to Ilar like that. What if once the curse was lifted he didn't want her anymore? If he said yes, it would only be out of his duty to protect his people. Surely, afterward, he would despise her.

"Is there no other way?" Ilar demanded. He saw her obvious displeasure in the plan. Her look tore out the remaining pieces of his heart and soul and smashed them into the ground. He felt hollow.

"The only way to get it to stop is to choose her as a lifemate—binding you forever," Cupid said, gasping. "In doing so, she'll be immortal. You'll never be rid of her."

Cupid chuckled despite himself, though he was still afraid of the ugly mortal putting her lips to him. If the other trolls ever discovered such a thing, he'd be ruined.

"Aye, you or another of your kind," Cupid said to Ilar. "It matters not who, only that it is done."

Ilar tensed. He couldn't stand to give her to someone else. But, if it was just a spell, what happened when the enchantment ended? Would she still feel so strongly? Would he? He'd never stopped to consider the influence the enchantment might be having on her. When she first came to him, her mortal prejudice had been overwhelming. Could he trust her human mind to have changed so quickly? And what of her human heart?

"What will happen if I don't?" Rhiannon asked.

"Then the spell will again grow and you will be sought after by every lycan for miles," Cupid said. He gave up his struggle and hung like a dead weight from Malak's firm grip. "Only when the spell is broken will the lycan see you for what you are—an ugly, horrible, mortal woman."

"You're awful. Hateful." Rhiannon rushed forward to the troll. Tears in her eyes, she tried to hit him.

Ilar caught her fist before it struck, though he too wanted nothing more than to kill the offensive little troll.

"You can always go home, my lady," the troll said, shivering against her anger, but much more welcoming of her fist than her lips. "There the lycan cannot smell you unless the portals open and the worlds merge. But you are mortal. You will not live that long."

Rhiannon jerked away from Ilar. Tears streamed down her face. She spun on her heels to face him. Staring up into his handsome features, she asked him, "So you did have to be with me to end the curse. It was all the enchantment's doing."

Rhiannon gasped at the pain searing through her and ran away from them, limping lightly on her ankle. Tears poured bitterly from her eyes and she sobbed them with great heaving breaths. Part of her had dared to hope Ilar wasn't with her for the enchantment but hearing Cupid's words only confirmed her worst fears. He only wanted her because of a mindless revenge spell.

She didn't stop running, not caring where she went. She prayed a giant dragon would swoop down from the sky and swallow her whole. Better dead in the belly of a dragon than back in the mortal world with a hole in her heart.

Ilar watched Rhiannon run away from them, knowing that she couldn't go anywhere he couldn't track her. His heart ran after her to see her dejection, but his legs stayed firmly planted. Turning to deal with the troll at hand, he said, "You've done it this time, Cupid."

"Does she truly think that it's only the enchantment that binds you to her?" Malak asked, surprised.

Ilar glanced at him, questioning. "How could she not think that? It's the truth."

"Ilar," Malak said. "I can't believe you haven't figured it out. Truly, if I thought you so dense, I would have told you sooner."

"What are you talking about, Malak?" Ilar asked, ignoring the squirming troll gripped in Malak's hand. His eyes churned with golden fire.

"You are immune to this troll's magic, Ilar," Malak stated. "You are immune to every trolls' magic. You were never under an enchantment. Every feeling has been your own."

Ilar frowned, doubtful, hopeful, not understanding.

"As have Rhiannon's," Malak continued. "When I received the immunity draught, I was drunk. I used it on myself and poured the rest on your head while you slept."

"You never said this to me." Ilar looked at his friend in disbelief.

"It wasn't important at the time. It was during the human battles. The next morning, we were attacked at our fort. I never thought to mention it before." Malak sighed. "Until smelling her, I had forgotten all about it."

A slow smile crept over Ilar's face. Without thinking, he darted down the mountainside as fast as his legs would carry him. Seeing Rhiannon limping down a path, her shoulders jerking with sobs, he grabbed her, moving to take her weight as he set her on the ground.

Rhiannon screamed in surprise, instantly fighting her assailant. Seeing Ilar's face beneath her tear-stained one, she fought harder, striking his chest.

"Let me go, Ilar. I'm going home," she yelled.

"You are home," he said, rolling his body over to subdue her beneath his weight. She blinked, confused. She stopped trying to hit him. Her lips were swollen with the thought of his kisses.

"This isn't amusing. I won't have your life destroyed to end a curse." Unable to stop her fingers, she lifted them to brush a soft piece of hair from his face, letting the long strands trail through her fingers. She lowered her hand, still holding it. Weakly, she said, "You deserve happiness."

"You truly believe that?" If he never let her up from him, he would be a happy man.

"Yes," she said. "I do."

Ilar leaned forward as if to kiss her. Rhiannon turned her face away and tightly closed her eyes. "Please, no, do not. I can't take anything more from you. I've fallen in love with you. Now, please, let me go before it gets worse. I know you only feel the spell. Please, Ilar, have pity on me."

"Never," he spat, forcing his lips to hers, crushing her with an all-powerful kiss that stole her breath and the rest of her heart. "I'll never let you go. You are mine, Rhian. Only mine. I choose here and now that you are forever my lifemate. Never shall it be undone."

Rhiannon blinked in confusion, her mouth opened in protest. She saw a golden shift purpling and cementing in his eyes, knowing he'd done something to bind him to her.

"No," she cried, closing her eyes, waiting to feel his rejection of her. "No, Ilar, you mustn't."

"It's too late." Slowly, he brushed his lips to hers, licking her mouth open to him. She gasped to feel his tenderness. She barely dared to hope as she met his piercing gaze. It was full of longing.

"You still want me?"

"I'll always want you. I have always wanted you.

Malak poured an immunity spell on me long ago—forgetting to mention it, of course. I'm unaffected by troll magic. Everything I have done and said has been from my heart. You, Lady Rhiannon of Weilshire, mortal, human, are this beast's heart. Now, what I would know is, can you love a *nieten*?"

"No," she answered. Ilar tensed. She smiled brightly at him, grabbing his face to pull him to her lips. "But I can love a lycan. I do love a lycan."

Ilar could not take his eyes from her. "I love you, Rhian, my wife, my lifemate, my heart. Together we shall live for an eternity."

Rhiannon moaned as he kissed her and didn't dare pull away as he began undoing the brooch at her shoulder, freeing a breast to his tenderly caressing mouth.

"Argh," came a growl. Rhiannon blinked to see a green piskie storming away from them. "Damned humans. Accursed lycans."

Rhiannon giggled, unafraid. Ilar snapped his teeth at the critter, causing a jolt of excitement in her chest. It ambled off as fast as it could run. Ilar grinned, devilish and handsome. He began kissing her neck, and she let him, trusting him completely. His teeth brushed up against her and she knew what he planned, could feel it. Lightly, he bit into her flesh, drinking from her, marking her as his as he fulfilled his primal need for her. Then, pulling back, he watched the wounds on her neck heal.

Rhiannon smiled up at him, her eyes heavy with longing. Ilar moved to kiss her, whispering, "Now you are as bound to me as I am to you."

Ilar lifted their tunics enough so they may join and still preserve some of his mate's endearing modesty. Rhiannon didn't care who saw them. She was only happy to be in his arms.

"Are you sure you wish to do this?" Ilar asked, doubtful, seeing what his wife's sister looked like. Agrona was positively horrible in her yards of white silk. He looked down at Rhiannon from where they hid, surprised that such two different creatures could be related. Cupid was bound and gagged behind them, squirming to be free.

"Yes, my love," Rhiannon said. "Just because she lacks beauty, doesn't mean she should lack love. Besides, this little troll owes us a favor."

Cupid grunted in protest as Rhiannon poked him in the ribs.

"What says you, Cupid? Do you help my sister or do you take a bath?" Rhiannon asked.

Cupid made a grunt that sounded much like 'help.'

Rhiannon nodded. Slowly, she stood, walking across the hall in her draping tunic attire to where Agrona sat. Agrona blinked in surprise to see her sister and quickly dashed at her teary eyes.

"Rhian?" she breathed. "We thought you were dead."

"No, I'm well. Better than well." Rhiannon sat on the bench. Lightly stroking back Agrona's wild hair, she plaited it for her as she spoke. "I've come to wish you happiness on your wedding day."

"It was very wicked of you to leave without sending word," Agrona said, her voice soft. They'd never been close. "I tried to tell father that you'd run off with one of the knights because he refused to let you marry."

"My absence couldn't be helped," Rhiannon said, her voice wry in its tone. She looked sidelong at Cupid. The troll's face was red with anger.

"I'm glad you're here, sister," Agrona put forth. "I think you should marry this man in my place. He's handsome and wants nothing to do with me."

"I wouldn't be so sure," Rhiannon said, standing. She smiled down at her sister's face. "I have to go now. Tell father I am well."

"But you have just arrived. Where have you been?" Agrona looked confused. Rhiannon handed her a missive.

"Here, give this to father," she said. "I'm sorry I can't stay to see you wed. But, I'm happy, ever so happy."

"I'm glad someone finally let you out of the tower." Agrona's expression shone with her sincerity.

Rhiannon motioned to Ilar. He stood beside her, his body also strangely attired to the gaping Agrona.

"This is my husband, Ilar," Rhiannon said, her love shining on her face. "With him I'm whole. Tell father when you see him. Don't let him worry. I am safe with him, but I may not be able to return."

Agrona nodded dutifully. Rhiannon rushed forward to hug her sister. Agrona grunted in surprise. When Rhiannon pulled back, a pink liquid soaked into the back of her sister's head. She smiled a secret smile. Agrona trembled, unaware of what was done.

"Come," Ilar said, pulling his wife away. "It works fast. We must be gone."

Rhiannon waved at her sister. Ilar grabbed Cupid and carried him hanging from one hand. Agrona was too dazed to notice the troll. As they rushed through the front entryway of the castle, a big man brushed past them, not seeing anything but his beautiful bride.

Cupid grumbled. The human knight rushed forward to press his future wife with kisses. Agrona gasped in amazement but melted into the man's arms. Cupid couldn't bear to watch as his Agrona was claimed by someone else.

Rhiannon smiled brightly, hugging herself to Ilar's waist. Her eyes shone with love for him, as did his for her. Without thought as to who watched them, she lifted on her toes and began kissing him freely. Cupid grunted in disgust. Glancing down at the mournful troll, before turning her lips to Ilar's once more, she said, "Now, open the portal, troll, and take us home."

The End

New York Times & *USA TODAY*
Bestselling Author

Michelle loves to travel and try new things, whether it's a paranormal investigation of an old Vaudeville Theatre or climbing Mayan temples in Belize. She believes life is an adventure fueled by copious amounts of coffee.

Newly relocated to the American South, Michelle is involved in various film and documentary projects with her talented director husband. She is mom to a fantastic artist. And she's managed by a dog and cat who make sure she's meeting her deadlines.

For the most part she can be found wearing pajama pants and working in her office. There may or may not be dancing. It's all part of the creative process.

COMPLIMENTARY EXCERPTS

TRY BEFORE YOU BUY!

Paranormal Fantasy Romance
Naughty Cupid Book Two

Cupid's livid. It's bad enough he made two people fall in love, but now thanks to King Larus, the whole Immortal Realm knows about it. There's only one thing a troll can do. Get Revenge.

Lady Mina and her sister are impoverished, starving, and their castle home is crumbling around their feet. With their father is dead, the servants have all fled and left them to fend for themselves in the middle of winter. Mina doesn't think things could get worse, until they're kidnapped and left as an offering to a handsome man-beast.

After Cupid caused a great disruption amongst his lycans by bringing an enchanted human to their realm, King Larus had to meet with the Council of Elders to tell what the troll had done. It should have been enough to stop future mischief. Or so he thought. Now he's trapped in the woods with two beautiful women—one whose madly in love with him and one who wants nothing more than to claw his eyes out. Larus is quickly learning not to underestimate a troll bent on revenge.

Excerpt

Curse the lycans.

Cupid's little black eyes flashed with an inner fire. And damn the council of immortal elders. So what if he took his vengeance out on Ilar by entrancing the whole Lycan Guard at Lycaon to one mortal woman? It's not like anyone had gotten hurt. Besides, Ilar, Commander of the Guard, deserved it for making fun of a noble troll— just as he deserved to be forced to lifemate to an ugly human woman.

Cupid shivered in disgust to think of how his plan had backfired. Ilar had fallen in love with the hideous mortal and they were living their fairy tale, happily ever after. It was disgustingly romantic. It was hideously repulsive. It was unbearable to think about.

Bah. Ach.

Now he had to listen to the other trolls tease him each time he saw them. They called him a cherub, a matchmaker, a rosy-faced babe who spread love and goodness throughout the two realms. If he had another basket of love darts left outside his cave door, he'd scream so loud the whole realm of magic would collapse in on itself.

Bah. Bah. Double bah.

Cupid hated the elders. He hated goodness and happiness. He hated Ilar and his ugly human lifemate, Rhiannon. He hated the council. He hated the realm of magic and the realm of mortals. He hated everyone and everything.

And, above all things, he hated love.

His humiliation wouldn't have been so widely known if the council of immortal elders hadn't been called forth. He blamed Larus, the elected king of the lycans, for that one. It was Larus's court at Lycaon that had been affected by his small enchantment prank. He merely made the mortal woman irresistible to the lycan kind and brought the whole court howling to their knees with lust.

But, could the lycan king let it go? No. He had to draw attention to the fact that Cupid had found love for Lord Ilar and Lady Rhiannon. He had to tell everyone who would listen to him that Cupid was personally responsible for Ilar's eternal happiness.

Now Cupid would never live his reputation down. First, he *accidentally* hit a man instead of a goat with a love dart, causing *one* couple to fall in love four hundred years ago, and now this. He was going to be branded for his immortal life as a matchmaker. It was beyond torture, beyond fair and right, beyond tolerable.

And, as far as Cupid could determine, it was King Larus who needed to pay for that.

To find out more about Michelle's books visit www.MichellePillow.com